STEP IN THE DARK

Under a façade of rural peace, hidden evil erupts in murder...

What riddles lie behind the doors of the normally sedate Ramsden Library and Scientific Society that could have led to the death of a pretty young librarian? What secrets were hidden in the rare and valuable books that appear to have been stolen? Why has the Society's historian suddenly disappeared? And what frightening treasure has the cleaning lady's delinquent son unearthed? Superintendent Pollard and Inspector Toye dig up the long-buried pasts of Ramsden's leading families and untangle the murky relationships of a secluded town and its tight-lipped citizenry.

STEP IN THE DARK

STEP IN THE DARK

by

Elizabeth Lemarchand

Dales Large Print Books
Long Preston, North Yorkshire,
BD23 4ND, England.

British Library Cataloguing in Publication Data.

Lemarchand, Elizabeth
    Step in the dark.

    A catalogue record of this book is
    available from the British Library

    ISBN   978-1-84262-586-6 pbk

First published in 1977

Copyright © 1976 by Elizabeth Lemarchand

Cover illustration © Arcangel Images

The moral right of the author has been asserted

Published in Large Print 2008 by arrangement with
Elizabeth Lemarchand, care of Watson, Little Ltd.

Dales Large Print is an imprint of Library Magna Books Ltd.

Printed and bound in Great Britain by
T.J. (International) Ltd., Cornwall, PL28 8RW

All the characters and events portrayed in this story are fictitious.

To all my friends
at the
Devon and Exeter Institution

Chief Characters

The Ramsden Literary and Scientific
  Society (Founded 1873)
The Athenaeum
6 Abbot's Green
Ramsden

Chairman: James Westlake, Esq, FSA, JP

Founder's Kin

Colin Escott – great-grandson
Daphne Escott – Colin's wife
Peter Escott – their son
Evelyn Escott – great-great-niece

Staff and Others

Alastair Habgood, DSO, FLA – Librarian
Laura Habgood – Alastair's wife
Clare Fenner – their niece
Annabel Lucas – Librarian's assistant

Flo Dibble – cleaner
Ernie Dibble – her son
Professor Henry Thornley, D.LITT, FSA –
  distinguished new member

Police

Detective-Inspector Cook, Ramsden CID
Detective-Inspector Gregory Toye, New
  Scotland Yard
Detective-Superintendent Tom Pollard,
  New Scotland Yard

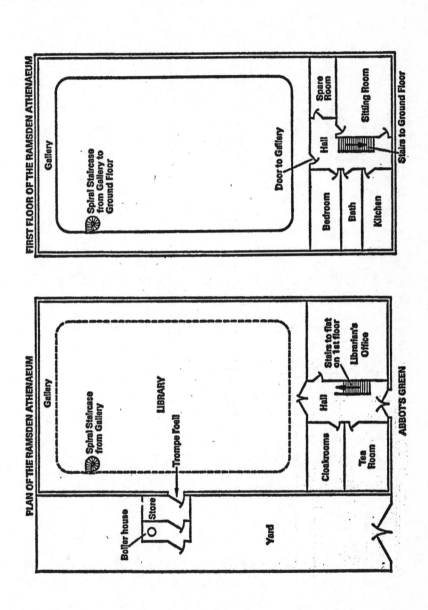

Chapter 1

On a November evening the Ramsden Literary and Scientific Society held a sherry party to celebrate its centenary at the Athenaeum, its headquarters in Abbot's Green.

Soon after six, Laura Habgood adjusted an ear-ring and came out of her bedroom in the Librarian's flat. This occupied the upper floor of the fifteenth-century gatehouse that formed the front section of the building.

'I'm going down,' she called to her husband, who was reading *The Times* in the sitting room. 'People turn up fantastically early.'

The Times crackled.

'Perhaps I'd better follow on,' Alastair Habgood replied reluctantly, hoisting himself up and retrieving his stick. A war injury thirty years earlier had left him with a permanently damaged left leg.

Laura went out of the front door of the flat, hoisted up her long skirt a few inches and ran down a short flight of stairs to the entrance hall. She gave a quick look round,

17

straightened a notice pinned crookedly on a board and went to the library. A rapid flicking of switches flooded the great room with light. It occupied the site of a former eighteenth-century house that had replaced the original mediaeval house and its courtyard. Evelyn Escott, founder of the Society, had bought the property, gutted it and converted it into the present impressive library. The windows were bricked up, lighting being provided by the fanlights in two cupolas in the roof. A narrow, encircling gallery gave access to the upper levels of shelving and was reached by means of a spiral staircase at the far end of the room and a door from the librarian's first-floor flat.

Old Evelyn's square, forceful countenance, framed in prolific facial hair, looked down on his achievement from his portrait over the fireplace. The forehead was prominent, the nose flattish and the lips thick. The very intelligent dark eyes were alight with the intoxication of nineteenth-century scientific progress, and the expression was one of unquestioning optimism.

Oblivious of past history, Laura Habgood checked over the trays of snacks she had prepared during the afternoon. On her husband's appointment to the librarianship in

1948, she had taken on the domestic responsibilities of the Athenaeum and carried them out with marked success ever since. Satisfied that everything was in order, she turned to greet two male members who had volunteered to preside at the bar.

'It looks smashing, Mrs H.,' one of them remarked, gazing round the library. 'Made for a party, this room.'

'If old Evelyn heard that, he'd turn in his grave,' remarked James Westlake, Chairman of the Trustees, coming up to the group. 'You must read the Minutes of the early meetings of the Trustees some time... The flowers are really magnificent, my dear,' he added, turning to Laura. 'I don't know how you do it.'

'Your chrysanthemums,' she reminded him, gratified.

By now there was a steady stream of arrivals, and James Westlake went over to the door to welcome them. Most people came in couples or small parties but a short stocky woman entered alone and was on the point of slipping unobtrusively past the Chairman when he caught her by the arm.

'Miss Evelyn Escott! First of the family to turn up! So glad you've been able to make it!'

She coloured a little, made a formal reply, then headed for the far end of the room.

In the hall Alastair Habgood was making conversation with Colin Escott, the founder's great-grandson, and his wife Daphne. Colin, bull-necked in a dinner jacket, and redolent of after-shave, appeared jocularly self conscious, and kept looking about him as he talked. Daphne Escott, impeccably groomed and with-it, combined conventional good looks with a blank expression. She finally broke in with a suggestion that they were monopolizing Mr Habgood and had better move on.

'I'm sure it's going to be a super party,' she said unconvincingly. 'Such a splendid lot of people here...'

As they moved on they ran into James Westlake who had emerged from the library. He greeted Daphne politely, Colin more briefly.

'Glad to see the family well represented,' he said. 'Your cousin, Miss Evelyn Escott, is here already. Peter coming along?'

'We left him in the bath,' Colin replied. 'No earthly reason why he couldn't be ready on time. He's coming on in his own car – or so he said.'

'What a crowd!' Daphne said, attempting

to introduce a more festive note. 'I'm sure it's going to be a splendid party. Come on, Colin.'

James Westlake bore down on Alastair Habgood. 'Where on earth's Professor Thornley?' he demanded. 'He ought to be here by now. Awkward if we have to start without him.'

As he spoke, the front door opened to admit a small, almost bald man with rimless spectacles, wearing a tweed overcoat and woollen muffler: a well-known Oxford social historian who had just joined the Ramsden Literary and Scientific Society for the research facilities afforded by its library. On catching sight of James Westlake, he raised a hand in greeting.

'Run it a bit fine, I'm afraid,' he said. 'Train was late.'

Edging him towards the cloakroom to deposit his overcoat and muffler, James Westlake assured the newcomer that there was plenty of time. Blast-off wasn't until half-past six, and they were always a few minutes late in starting.

The library was now full to congestion point. People were circulating with difficulty, glasses of sherry in their hands, and there was a babel of conversation. At twenty minutes to seven, having deposited Professor Thornley with Alastair Habgood, James Westlake made his way to the librarian's table and surveyed the scene before him. He was a tall man in his middle sixties, with thick white hair shaggy at the back and a countryman's weathered face. Taking up an ivory gavel, one of Old Evelyn's legacies, he hammered vigorously. The noise gradually died down and the crowd orientated itself in his direction.

'Fellow members and guests of RLSS,' he began, looking round with unconcealed pride and satisfaction, 'it is with very great pleasure...'

A young man in a light suit with fashionably wide lapels and sporting an eye-catching tie slipped into the room and took up a position next to Annabel Lucas, Alastair Habgood's assistant. She made a slightly provocative movement of her left shoulder as they exchanged glances. He responded with the lift of an eyebrow.

'On this notable and happy occasion,' James Westlake was saying, 'our thoughts turn, of course, to our founder, Evelyn Escott, whose munificent endowment of RLSS with the freehold of this building was followed by the equally munificent bequest of his personal library.'

'Old bastard!' muttered Colin Escott. 'Robbing the family for his ruddy Society.'

Several heads turned. Daphne kicked him on the ankle.

'...pleasure of having members of the family with us this evening,' pursued the Chairman. 'Mr and Mrs Colin Escott, with their son Peter, all keeping up the link. Miss Evelyn Escott is here, too: great-great-niece and namesake of our Founder. She has recently come back to her native town, to spend what we hope will be a very happy retirement, after working for many years in London. Most appropriately she is going to write a long-overdue history of our Society.'

There was a polite spatter of applause as the Chairman bowed in Evelyn Escott's direction. She had made no attempt to join her relatives and was standing by the fireplace under her great-great-uncle's portrait.

'God!' Peter Escott remarked audibly to his neighbour. 'It only wanted this.'

Annabel Lucas managed to convey complete agreement while remaining outwardly impassive. Lounging against a book-stack with folded arms, he eyed her appraisingly. Distinct possibilities, he decided, but definitely not his type. Too angular, and the

23

sort of lips that became a thin line when she was off guard...

A perceptive observer would have detected resemblances to their forebear in the faces of the Escotts present. Colin, a successful Ramsden estate agent, had inherited the massive jowl and blunt nose, but shrewdness rather than the thirst for truth looked out of his eyes; and he had the stamp of good living and a philistine bonhomie. In Peter Escott, the Founder's prominent brow topped a narrower face with similar, if less luxuriant, sideburns. He looked intelligent and disgruntled; and was a salaried employee in his father's firm. Evelyn Escott was the sole survivor of an unsuccessful junior branch of the family. In her the strong lines of old Evelyn's face were softened by sensitive features and a frame of lightly curling hair, hardly as yet touched by grey.

'And so, members and guests,' the Chairman concluded buoyantly, 'I give you our Founder, all benefactors past and present, and the Ramsden Literary and Scientific Society's next hundred years!'

Glasses were raised amid loud acclamation and laughter.

'Blah!' Colin Escott commented under cover of the noise. 'Look, there are the Med-ways. Let's join up.'

Now that the formal part of the proceedings was over, the gathering began to fragment into small groups. Friends hailed friends and members of the Society's various sections plunged into discussion of common interests. Prominent among these was the recent discovery of mediaeval foundations in the course of demolition work in the town centre. The library rang with angry denunciations of the apathy of the Council and the blind commercialism of property development companies. More temperately, the Natural History section debated the reliability of an alleged sighting of a mealy redpoll in the district. It was a lively and attractive scene, the formal dignity of the great room relieved by bright lights, the bronze and gold of massed chrysanthemums and autumn foliage and the kaleidoscopic colour pattern of the women's dresses, caught up and repeated in the spines of the thousands of books on the shelves.

After a time James Westlake managed to extricate himself and rejoined Alastair Habgood and Professor Thornley.

'Impressive set-up,' the latter remarked, looking around. 'I gather this room was old Escott's brainchild?'

'Yes, it was,' James Westlake replied. 'He gutted the Georgian extension grafted on to the gatehouse and rebuilt it to provide this library. Against his architect's advice, of course. It nearly sank the Society, in due course.'

'Maintenance, you mean?'

'Maintenance, and heating and cleaning costs. The Trustees were on the point of packing in the whole show after the war.'

'I expect you've heard how our Chairman saved the situation?' Alastair Habgood put in.

'Found the manuscript of that hitherto unknown Donne sonnet, didn't you?' the Professor asked. 'How did it happen? It must have been an incredible experience.'

James Westlake briefly explained how, on demobilization, he had returned to farm his small family estate near Ramsden. In the course of the war the Society's Board of Trustees had become depleted, and he had agreed to become a member and help to arrive at a decision on whether it was practicable to carry on. After lengthy discussion, the Trustees came to the conclusion that the only course open to them was the winding-up of the Society, and instructed their legal adviser to look into the procedure involved.

'Soon afterwards, I came along here in a nostalgic mood one afternoon,' James Westlake said. 'Local history's one of my hobbies, and I thought I'd have a look round to see if there were any reference books, or whatever, that I might be able to buy in. The building was in an appalling state: damp patches on the walls, the roof leaking in places and that awful stink of dry rot. I started going through a cupboard stuffed with heaven knows what and found a lot of old local maps. The Donne manuscript was in with them.'

'Good Lord!' ejaculated Professor Thornley. 'Was it much damaged?'

'Surprisingly, very little. Of course I couldn't positively identify it on the spot, but my local history hobby has made me fairly familiar with seventeenth-century scripts, and the signature was plain enough. And there was the sonnet form and the Donnish title: "A starre called Wormwood". When I came to, I packed the thing in what clean protective wrapping I could find, and the next day I took it up to a chap I knew at the British Museum.'

'Fetched the earth at auction, didn't it?'

'A hundred thousand. When we'd got our breath back we roped in assorted experts, and got cracking as fast as the post-war building restrictions allowed. And we were lucky enough to find Habgood here.' James Westlake grinned appreciatively at the librarian. 'What's more, he'd had the foresight to acquire an absolutely invaluable wife with a domestic science diploma, who's shouldered all that side of the business for us ever since.'

'Nice work,' Professor Thornley summed up. 'I remember the furore in the literary world at the time. Then I suppose you decided to reorganize the library for local environmental studies?'

'Exactly.'

Around them the party was gathering momentum. Laura Habgood contrived to keep an eye on the circulation of drinks and snacks while chatting to members. She also unobtrusively watched her husband, now deep in discussion with James Westlake and Professor Thornley, and wished that the trio would go and find somewhere to sit. If Alastair stood about much longer, his leg would start playing up.

As she registered this thought, James Westlake, who took his official duties seriously, disengaged himself for the polite formality of introducing the Founder's kin present and the distinguished new member. Evelyn Escott was temporarily lost in the crowd, but he located Colin and his wife and son and propelled them towards Professor Thornley.

This encounter hung fire badly, owing to the fact that the persons concerned were on quite different wavelengths. Colin, aware of being out of his depth, took refuge in a series of facetious remarks about his ancestor, punctuated by guffaws. Daphne, puzzled by the speculative wonder on Professor Thornley's face, tried to help out by contributing a series of well-meant fatuities. Peter Escott remained sulkily mute. Finally he abruptly cut in, ignoring his parents.

'Are you sold on decorative plasterwork, by any chance, sir?' he asked. 'We've got some quite decent ceilings up in the gatehouse. I'll take you along, if you like.'

Professor Thornley, grasping at a straw, avowed keen interest, if combined with limited knowledge of the subject, and was led away. James Westlake made his apologies and went off. The Escotts looked at each other with relief and uncomprehending shrugs.

'Peter's useful now and again,' Colin conceded. 'Here, since we've come to this lousy show we may as well be seen. We seem to be part of the entertainment. Better have a word with dear Cousin Evelyn, I suppose, for the look of the thing.'

They began to make their way through the gathering, pausing to talk to various acquaintances. Suddenly they found themselves face to face with Evelyn Escott.

'Why, see who's here!' Colin exclaimed in mock astonishment. 'If it isn't Cousin Evelyn, the budding authoress!'

Evelyn looked at the couple, aware of being baited. Her self-confidence began to ebb. She suddenly felt that her mass-produced frock was ill-fitting and that her shoes were wrong.

'Good evening,' she said politely.

'Such a crowd!' Daphne contributed. 'All madly excited about birds and things.'

'Found any juicy scandals about the old boy to put in your book?' Colin inquired. 'That's the stuff for a best seller.'

'In the unlikely event of your reading it, you'd find it disappointing, I'm afraid,' she replied, and moved on.

To her annoyance, she felt ridiculously near to tears. Her cousins' unconcealed contempt had dowsed the small glow kindled by the Chairman's public recognition. Because of her long absence from Ramsden, she knew few people at the party, and a sense of being wretchedly and conspicuously alone engulfed her. Perhaps it she took down a book and pretended to be absorbed in it, people wouldn't notice that she was on her own.

As she made for the nearest shelves a hand on her shoulder made her start. She swung round to find herself looking up at James Westlake.

'Run you to earth at last, Miss Escott,' he said, smiling down at her. 'I couldn't see you just now when I took your cousins along to meet Professor Thornley, our new VIP member. You must meet him, too, of course. Young Peter's just taken him up to have a look at the ceilings, but they'll be down again soon. You'll be around, won't you?'

Once again aware of rising colour at this unexpected attention from the Chairman, Evelyn struggled to appear composed.

'Oh, thank you, Mr Westlake,' she replied. 'I'd like to meet him. Yes, I'll be around somewhere.'

'Good. See you again shortly, then.'

He was gone and she was alone once more, but the sense of unhappy and despised isolation had evaporated. On impulse she headed for the spiral staircase, and went up to the gallery. Resting her hands on its balustrade, she contemplated the scene below, but her thoughts had reverted to the cramping poverty of her early days and its bitter frustrations.

Trying to hang on to Escott status by our fingernails, she thought, while Colin's father and mother pretended we weren't there... How extraordinarily it is that after fighting my way into good jobs, and ending up with more money then I ever dreamt of, the only thing I really want is to be accepted here in Ramsden as an Escott in old Evelyn's tradition. To be somebody in RLSS.

The cruellest of all her early frustrations had been leaving school at sixteen for a cheap secretarial training, instead of going on to a university in due course. Even now a familiar angry sense of injustice rose up in her, but she brushed it aside, heartened by the Chairman's appreciation. Recalled to the present and looking down, she caught sight of him demonstrating the *trompe-l'œil*, a cleverly painted set of bookshelves forming a door leading through a small storage space to the boiler house. Nearby, another new friend, Alastair Habgood, was sitting on a sofa with some members, examining a large illustrated book. Nox, the Habgoods' small black cat, appeared to be sharing their interest from a vantage point on the top of a book stack.

Evelyn's eyes moved on. Her expression hardened at the sight of Annabel Lucas engaged in badinage with an elderly man who was displaying a tendency to paw. She disliked Annabel, accurately sensing that Peter Escott was in the habit of mocking at her with the girl. Her own antipathy to Peter went deep, fed by resentment at his having had the university education denied herself. She was suddenly riled at the thought of his playing the knowledgeable host to Professor Thornley, and seized with a desire to assert her family status and genuine interest in the building.

She surfaced abruptly to find that a middle-aged couple had joined her. The woman was saying how attractive the library looked from the gallery. '...Really, we're most awfully lucky to have a place like this for the Society's HQ,' she went on.

Evelyn warmed to her, and on impulse disclosed her own identity. The couple's instant interest was gratifying. They introduced themselves as Alan and Barbara Langley, RLSS members who had recently joined on moving to the area. In the course of conversation a question about the history of the Athenaeum suggested an idea to Evelyn. It transpired that they had not yet seen the famous ceilings in the Habgoods' flat, and her offer to act as guide was eagerly accepted. She escorted them round the gallery, enjoying the sense of involvement and hoping that Peter Escott would still be in the flat. It would be satisfying to demostrate publicly that she had an equally good – if not better – knowledge of the Athenaeum's features of architectural interest.

As they went in she caught a glimpse of Peter disappearing into the Habgoods' sitting room, and through the half-open door she could see Professor Thornley occupied in making a sketch of a section of ceiling. Several other people were wandering around, and on hearing her conversation with the Langleys, they asked if they might tack on to the escorted tour.

'Please do,' she said, feeling gratified. 'I'd be only too glad. What is so interesting about these ceilings is that they show the progressive development of local ornamental plasterwork over about two centuries. Let's start here, in the bathroom. Shall I stand in the doorway, as there isn't much room?... Well, this is an example of early sixteenth-century work. You see that the panels are defined by single ribs, and based on squares. There are central bosses, and the only ornamentation is a simple Tudor rose.'

As she talked, Evelyn was at pains to enunciate clearly, and make her voice carry in the direction of the sitting room. After answering some questions, she moved her party on to the kitchen, and began to point out the elaboration of panel ribbing by the seventeenth-century pargeters.

About five minutes later, from the Habgoods' bedroom, she saw the two men emerge from the sitting room and go towards the stairs. Without hurrying too obviously, she speeded up her party and shortly afterwards returned to the library herself. Almost at once she was swept up with cheerful informality by James Westlake, and led towards the small, almost bald man with rimless spectacles whom she had earlier observed with interest from a distance.

'Here's another member of the Founder's family, Professor,' he said. 'Miss Evelyn Escott – his great-great-niece, to be exact – who's writing the history of the Society for us.'

'Aha!' The resignation on Professor Thornley's face promptly vanished. 'The lady who is so well-informed about your Ramsden pargeters! I must admit to listening-in just now, Miss Escott. I'm glad to have the chance of a chat with you. Tell me, what sources are you drawing on for this history of yours?'

James Westlake faded away, leaving them together. Aware that something about the Professor invited confidences, Evelyn plucked up her courage. 'Quite honestly, I'm not sure that I'm capable of writing it at all,' she heard herself saying, with a sense of relief at putting her secret fear into words. 'You see, I'm only self-educated. I never went to a university.'

'That, my dear lady,' he replied with emphasis, 'could well be an advantage. Shall we find a seat? I understand from your excellent librarian that the Society's Minute Books provide an unusually full record. A great old chap, your forebear,' he added with a chuckle as they sat down. 'I was enchanted to hear from the Chairman that his last conscious moment was devoted to Braithewaite's *Encyclopaedia of Extinct Mammalia.*'

The centenary party, as more than one member remarked to Laura Habgood, had gone like a bomb. It was nice to get so many congratulations on the flowers and the food, but she had had a long, hard day and began to wish that people would go. At last the trickle of departures became a steady stream and she decided to make an unobtrusive start on the clearing-up. It was out of the question to let Flo Dibble, the cleaner, be confronted with a complete shambles on arrival the next morning.

The Chairman, always a tower of strength at this depressing stage of a party, had gone off to give Professor Thornley and Alastair dinner at an hotel, but Laura was heartened by the number of volunteer helpers who presented themselves. Within a short time she had the operation organized. The hired wine glasses were being collected and packed up, left-over food sorted and removed to the kitchen and furniture restored to its normal position. Evelyn Escott showed herself particularly deft and brisk. Laura wondered briefly why she was looking so starry-eyed, and was surprised to see Peter Escott stacking folding chairs and taking them to the store, instead of sloping off at the earliest possible moment with his objectionable parents. With some irritation she noticed Annabel Lucas's blatant come-hither tactics towards him, but these were apparently being ignored.

In half an hour the job was done, and the library largely restored to its normal appearance. Reiterating her thanks, Laura manoeuvred towards the front door those helpers who had stayed to the bitter end. She dropped the catch with a sigh of relief. All that remained now was to take a final look round and lock the library door. This done, she went wearily upstairs with the key. Nox preceded her with tail indignantly erect, indicative of a long overdue supper.

Chapter 2

The chrysanthemums and autumn foliage were still bright patches of colour when Evelyn Escott went into the library the following morning, but all other traces of the centenary party had vanished. There was a spring in her step. In her case were the invaluable guide lines and lists of reference books that Professor Thornley had given her. Even more than this, he had insisted on her having his address in case she needed further advice. She put down the case on the table in her favourite bay and went up to the gallery to fetch the earliest volume of the Trustees' Minutes. Noticing Annabel Lucas was at the card index cabinet, she wondered briefly where Alastair Habgood was. Wednesday morning was not normally one of Annabel's library times.

She had already worked through the earliest Minutes, from the initial enthusiasm and grandiose schemes of 1873 to the first faint intimations of restiveness under the Founder's autocratic chairmanship. Then had come his sudden death from a heart attack in 1895, and the carefully recorded eulogies with their discreet references to high ideals and strong personality. Now, before the year was out, the floodgates were opening. Evelyn read with amusement that the playing of chess, draughts, backgammon and halma were at last authorized by the Trustees, albeit with the proviso that gaming for stakes in any part of the Athenaeum was strictly prohibited. Then 1897 saw an even more revolutionary development: a room in the gatehouse was set apart for smoking!

What would have happened if old Evelyn had lived much longer, she speculated, glancing up at the portrait over the fireplace? Just as well that he hadn't: it was all rather pathetic as well as comic.

It was not long before she came upon the first reference to the financial difficulties that were to bedevil the Ramsden Literary and Scientific Society for the next fifty years. In 1898 the annual accounts were in deficit for the first time. The Treasurer reported that repairs to the roof had been a great deal more costly than expected. Some sharp exchanges followed. Reading between the lines, it was clear that the work ought to have been put in hand much earlier. Perhaps old

Evelyn had flatly refused to admit that the building was developing defects? At the same meeting there was an acrimonious discussion about the disappointing sum realized by the sale of the Founder's stamp collection, which he had bequeathed to the Society with his books. The Chairman had replied, with easily imaginable asperity, that Mr Escott had presumably disposed of some of the more valuable items before his death, and that the Trustees could rest assured that expert advice had been taken about the most appropriate way of putting the collection on the market.

At this point Evelyn decided to break off for lunch, and took her sandwiches to the room where tea and coffee were available for the Society's members. On the way there she ran into Laura Habgood, and learned that Alastair was having a bad day with his leg and had been obliged to knock off.

'It was all that standing about last night,' Laura said. 'He just can't take it. But he'll be perfectly OK tomorrow, after a rest today and his dope. It was lucky that Annabel was able to come in this morning as well as this afternoon.'

Evelyn sent a sympathetic message. After finishing her snack she went out to do some domestic shopping, then returned to the library, with a pleasant afternoon in prospect. She had hardly sat down, however, when she felt a sudden chill: someone had obviously been examining her notebooks and papers. They were disarranged, and in one case were actually out of order.

She thought back rapidly. Two men had been reading in the library when she went out to lunch, but she discounted them at once. No, it was that odious Annabel Lucas, of course, probably hoping to find something to laugh at with Peter Escott. She reddened with anger, while recognizing that there was nothing she could do about it, beyond making sure that there were no further opportunities of the kind.

Apart from this annoying discovery, the afternoon passed peacefully; and it was nearly five o'clock when the recurring image of tea made her feel that it was really time to knock off. She would just check one reference in the *Ramsden Recorder,* the town's weekly newspaper, and then go home.

The *Recorder* dated from the late eighteenth century, and the Society had a valuable unbroken run of its issues, bound up annually in large, unwieldy volumes. These were kept in a bay with specially designed shelving. Evelyn went over to it, and with some difficulty managed to get down the year she wanted. As she opened it on the table, she chanced to look up: Annabel Lucas was sitting at the librarian's table, holding a book by its spine in both hands and shaking it as if expecting something to drop out. While there was nothing particularly remarkable in this, Evelyn was forcibly struck by a kind of furtiveness in the operation, and the impression was reinforced by Annabel's quick look in her own direction. She hastily pretended to be absorbed in the *Recorder,* turning its flimsy pages as if searching for some item. Her professional experience, however, had included responsibility for a roomful of typists, and she was adept at unobtrusive observation.

One book after another was taken up and shaken. Then two things happened at once: a small flat object shot across the table on to the floor, and the door opened to admit Laura Habgood.

'Alastair's much better, thank goodness,' she said. 'He wants you to bring his letters up for him to sign before you go.'

Annabel, on her feet in a flash, had come forward and was standing over the small flat object on the carpet.

'Oh, fine,' she said. 'I'm so glad. I've done the letters. I'll be up in just a minute, when I've put these books back.'

As Laura disappeared again, she stooped down, picked something up and reached for her handbag.

Useless to challenge her, Evelyn thought. Whatever she was up to, she'd simply say she was looking for a missing index card or something. She might complain about me, too...

The possibility of this was so unpleasant that she hastily plunged into speech to allay any suspicion of having snooped. 'You must have had a busy day, with Mr Habgood out of action,' she said.

Annabel looked round from a bookshelf. 'There hasn't been much doing, actually. Hardly anybody's been in today. Just routine jobs and whatever. You know. Would you mind switching off the lights when you come out?'

She collected her things and hurried off.

As Evelyn followed, curiosity impelled her to find out what books had been investigated so carefully. She had noted exactly where Annabel had replaced them, and paused to look. She found herself staring at the six volumes of Braithewaite's *Encyclo-*

paedia of Extinct Mammalia.

A series of facts began to link up in her mind. Professor Thornley's amusement at old Evelyn's having expired while actually reading this formidable work had led her to make a note of the incident. She had also recorded the surprise felt at the absence of valuable stamps believed to be included in his collection. Without any doubt, Annabel had read her notes during the lunch hour... At any rate, something had drawn the girl's attention to the *Encyclopaedia:* it was inconceivable that anything in the day's work in the library had involved taking down all six volumes and examining them. And what was more, she had secreted something which had fallen out of one of them.

She shan't get away with whatever it is, Evelyn thought angrily, feeling proprietorial towards the Society's assets and activated, to a greater extent than she realized, by personal dislike.

She slipped out into the hall and stood listening. Conversation was safely in progress upstairs. The door of the librarian's office was open, and Annabel's handbag lay on the desk. In a matter of seconds Evelyn had opened it and found a small semi-transparent envelope tucked into an inner pocket. She removed it, and was back in the hall on the way to the cloakroom as footsteps approached the top of the staircase. There was just time to establish the incredible fact that the envelope did, in fact, contain stamps, before oddly muted voices became audible outside the door. Her mind reeling, Evelyn fancied that she caught her own name, but perhaps she had imagined it…

Laura Habgood came in briskly, followed by Annabel. 'I was just saying that there's a House Committee on Monday, Miss Escott,' she said. 'The redecoration of this room's coming up, among other things. Same again, do you think, or would it be nice to have a change?'

Evelyn did her best to give a coherent answer, every fibre of her being intent on Annabel, who had put on a coat and was scrutinizing her make-up in a mirror. Would she start hunting for cosmetics in her bag and discover her loss? Apparently her face passed muster, and she moved towards the door.

'I must dash,' she said. 'I've got to drop in the car for its MOT test and the garage will be shutting.'

They followed her into the hall, Laura still discussing the redecorations programme.

By a miracle the telephone began to ring in the flat, and she dived for the stairs, breaking off in mid-sentence. 'Sorry,' she called over her shoulder, 'I don't want Alastair to get up.'

Evelyn opened the front door, willing Annabel to follow her. As it shut behind them both, she released a pent-up breath of relief. They parted with brief good-nights, and Evelyn set off on foot, her ears straining for the sound of Annabel's car being driven out of the Athenaeum yard. At last she heard it emerge, and the slam of the double doors. Finally it drove away towards the town.

Now at last she could take stock of the extraordinary situation into which she had so recklessly precipitated herself. The first thing was to get home and look at the stamps properly. It was unfortunate that she knew virtually nothing about philately, but there must be books about it in the public library. She would go round there first thing tomorrow morning. Of course, if they turned out to be very ordinary stamps, nothing further need be done, which would be a relief in one way. But at the back of her mind Evelyn knew that it would also be a bitter disappointment. It was beginning to dawn on her that she could be the means of restoring a lost fortune to the Society. One sometimes read of rare stamps fetching a fabulous sum at auctions...

Her home was the first of a small row of Victorian cottages that had survived in a residential road of big Edwardian houses and gardens. Being at the end of the row, hers had the advantage of greater privacy, its front door leading off a lane. As she turned into the latter, her mind was conjuring up a delectable vision of being thanked for her discovery by the Board of Trustees.

The violent thrust between her shoulders and the sensation of falling helplessly forward happened without the slightest warning. The objective world suddenly contracted to contact with hard muddy ground. In her sheer bewilderment at experiencing brutal force for the first time in her life, it took her a second or so to realize what had happened. Then she grasped frantically for her handbag. It had gone.

The shock of the discovery brought her to her feet, and she leaned helplessly against the cottage wall, looking desperately to right and left. No one was to be seen. A car flashed unheeding past the end of the lane, emphasizing her isolation. Remembering thankfully that she always carried her latchkey in an inside pocket, she managed to let herself into the cottage and struggled to the telephone to dial 999. Nothing mattered, absolutely nothing but getting her bag back.

But no sooner had she put the call through and sunk on to a chair when she felt appalled at what she had done. Without consulting anyone she was involving the Society in the most dreadful publicity, perhaps quite unnecessarily. Suppose the stamps were practically worthless? If only she had waited to put the whole story before Alastair Habgood. She realized that she was shivering uncontrollably. Before she could collect her thoughts, a car turned into the lane.

The two policemen were large men who seemed to crowd her tiny sitting room to suffocation point. They were kind and helpful, concerning themselves at first about whether she needed medical attention. The young constable was then dispatched to the kitchen to make her a cup of tea while Sergeant Mills of the Ramsden Constabulary questioned her minutely. He was sandy-haired, with sharp grey eyes that she felt were boring into her.

'You say you didn't hear anybody following you on the way home, or see the chap who knocked you over,' he said. 'Did you get any

49

idea if there was more than one person in on it?'

Evelyn shut her eyes and tried to think.

'I don't think so. I didn't hear footsteps running away, or anything. It all happened so quickly.'

Sergeant Mills nodded. 'Now, if you'd just describe the handbag and what was in it, Madam?'

'It wasn't an expensive bag,' she began, still agonizingly undecided about the stamps. 'A dark brown synthetic one, medium-sized, with handles. There was a red purse inside with about a pound in small change, I think. A pen, and my diary, and a shopping list. Oh, and a few stamps. I can't think of anything else.'

She held her breath. If he asked about the stamps she would have to tell the truth, of course.

Sergeant Mills showed no interest in them.

'Very sensible of you to carry your latch-key in an inside pocket, Madam,' he remarked. 'I wish all you ladies would do the same. Real careless with your handbags, some of you are.'

'Do you think there's any chance of getting mine back?' she asked him anxiously.

It struck Sergeant Mills as surprising that she should be so concerned about a cheap bag with next to nothing in it, but he replied encouragingly.

'I'm afraid there's not much hope of seeing your purse again, and maybe not your pen either. But the bag could turn up. A chap who's done a snatch usually gets rid of it quick, once he's cleaned out any valuables or cash. Chucks it over a wall or dumps it in a dustbin. Anyone finding it often brings it along to us, though. We'll contact you at once, of course, if it turns up. We'll take a look in the gardens just round here right away.'

He rose to go, advising a good hot bath in case she was stiff after her fall, and some aspirin.

'A nasty experience for you,' he said. 'It could have been a lot worse, though, couldn't it? Suppose you'd cashed a cheque at the bank today?'

Evelyn managed a rather wan smile as she thanked him.

Ernie Dibble watched the police car coast slowly along the road from the cover of some shrubs in the garden of the house opposite. He was disappointed and puzzled. His first mugging hadn't gone the way of the ones in the papers. He'd got the old cow's bag all right, but why hadn't she yelled blue murder instead of just lying there, then getting up and going into the house as though nothing had happened? She'd got the fuzz along fast enough, but there'd been no siren on the car or lights flashing. Not that he hadn't got his escape route lined up, over the wall at the back.

Finally he gave up and emerged cautiously. Ramsden born and bred, he knew the town like the back of his hand, and made his way unremarked through the streets to the grave-yard of the parish church. A footpath cutting through it was deserted at this hour, and after a quick look round he dived behind a large box tomb. In the light of a conveniently situated lamp, he eagerly opened the handbag.

His inflated expectations took a hard knock. No notecase, bulging with five pound notes. No keys, opening up thrilling possibili-ties. No valuables, and only loose coins in the purse. Even in the pocket with a zip-fastener there were only a few stamps. Deciding that they were foreign stamps, he transferred them to the pocket of his anorak for his kid brother, together with the purse and the fountain pen. He found a leaflet about some meeting at the place in Abbot's Green where his mum cleaned, and a diary with a name and address in it. There was nothing else. He sat back gloomily on his heels.

Ernie was an under-sized fourteen, with a peaky face and mousy hair. Nine years earlier, his father, an unskilled labourer, had walked out, leaving his wife with two small boys, and successfully eluding all attempts by the welfare services to trace him. Flo Dibble was a scant five feet but what she lacked in inches she more than made up for in will power and energy. From the day of her desertion these qualities were concentrated on what she called 'living right and proper'. The boys were brought up in an atmosphere of unremitting hard work, economy and respectability. She was so dominant in their lives that Ernie had only just, in his fifteenth year, arrived at breaking-out point. The Ramsden Comprehensive School had offered him a variety of constructive outlets, but they were either beyond his capacity or too communal for his taste. Gang activities had no appeal for him, and his first serious attempt to assert his independence had taken the form of this single-handed incursion into petty crime.

At first, as he rocked to and fro on his heels, disappointment at his meagre haul blotted out everything else. But a hard life had taught him to compensate. Gradually the fact that he had pulled off his first snatch began to bolster his ego. As footsteps approached, he squared his shoulders. As they drew near, he leaped out, in imagination...

High overhead the church clock chimed the first quarter. Ernie decided that he had better make tracks for home. His mum would be back from her office cleaning job in an hour's time, and she'd blow her bloody top if he hadn't come in. No sense in asking for trouble, even if he had knocked an old woman down and got her bag. Most people had gone home to an evening meal by now, and he had no difficulty in pushing Evelyn Escott's handbag into one of a stack of cardboard containers put out for the refuse collectors at the back entrance of a shop. He was now free to concentrate on essentials. After study of a display card, he went into a snack bar and bought a large, expensive ice-cream. He walked along briskly, slowly savouring its delectable sweetness and creaminess, reminding himself that he owed it to his enterprise and guts. Feeling jaunty, he diverged from the direct route home to stroll round Abbot's Green. It was a quiet sort of place, he told himself, and the lights weren't all that bright. Suppose there was a chance of another bash?

Apart from a man some distance ahead of him who was walking away round the far side of the Green, there was no one about. Ernie swaggered along, pausing to try the door of a solitary parked car. It was locked. He kicked its nearside front wheel and went on. He had once been to the Athenaeum with his mum, and now paused outside its front door. The big brass handle she was always shooting her mouth about shone in the light of the street lamp close by. On impulse he stepped forward and tried it. It turned easily. The door opened and, amazed at his own daring, he slipped inside.

He was in the hall, with all the notice boards on the walls. He could see quite well, as some light was coming down the stairs. He stood sniffing delicious cooking smells that made his mouth water. Moving very cautiously, he tried several doors unsuccessfully, then advanced on the one which he remembered led into the big room with the books. It had an iron ring hanging down instead of a proper handle, and slipping his hand through this he turned it gently.

To his horror, a latch shot up on the inside with a hideous clatter. As he froze, there was a funny sort of scrambling noise inside the room, followed by somebody screeching and calling out. Then some small thuds, and a big one. There was the sound of a door closing very quietly. Terrified by what sounded like a car drawing up outside, he pressed against the wall, trembling with terror. The noise stopped and, throwing caution to the winds, he opened the front door and ran for it. Peering out from the bushes in the centre of Abbot's Green, he could not see a car, and decided that it must have driven off. He stayed crouching on the wet ground for what felt like a lifetime.

Far away, small and faint, came the seven strokes of the hour from the clock in the tower of the parish church, but he still dared not move. At the sound of another car he waited with his heart in his mouth. It came nearer and nearer, and finally a Mini turned into the yard at the side of the Athenaeum. At the same moment, the front door opened, letting out a shaft of light, and a woman hurried round to the yard. A girl was getting out of the car and they hugged each other. Tears of self-pity sprang to Ernie's eyes as he suddenly thought of the reception awaiting him on his belated return. He watched the two women shut the yard doors and go into the house, before emerging cautiously on the far side of the bushes and starting reluctantly for his home.

After the police had gone, Evelyn Escott realized for the first time just how shaken and exhausted she was feeling. She had eaten nothing except a few sandwiches since breakfast, but the idea of food was nauseating. The thought of struggling round to the Athenaeum to tell Alastair Habgood of her probably ill-judged action and the appalling disaster that had followed left her paralysed. It was with overwhelming relief that she remembered he would be in no state to listen to her story after a bad day and the large doses of painkillers he was obliged to take on these occasions. In any case, nothing more could be done tonight. The police had been informed. She would go round the very first thing the next morning, arriving with the cleaning woman at half-past seven. Laura had once said that she came down every day to let her in then...

Presently she roused herself to heat some milk, then drank it with a great effort. She really must pull herself together, she thought miserably. Perhaps the best thing was to have a hot bath and go to bed. Take some aspirin, as the policeman had suggested. Try not to think what she might have lost the Society. Of the story getting out, and the publicity ... the sort of things the Colin Escotts would say about her ... of having to resign because it was so unbearable.

She slept very little, unsuspected bruises and jolts from her fall asserting themselves. The night, too, turned wet and stormy, rain lashing against her window like handfuls of flung gravel. At half-past six she was glad to get up and dress. Now that zero hour was nearly upon her she felt almost relieved and managed to eat a little breakfast before she started out – muffled in mackintosh and rain hood and struggling to keep up an umbrella against the driving wind and rain.

The streets were almost deserted and she met only a few hurrying figures, dressed, like herself, for the weather. Cleaning women going to their jobs, she thought, and found herself envying the simplicity of their lives, free from the sort of ambition that had made her struggle for the unattainable all her days.

Presently she turned into Abbot's Green. It was more sheltered here and she made better progress. She saw that the double doors into the Athenaeum's yard at the side of the building were partly open. Of course, Annabel hadn't shut them properly, and the high wind had forced them apart. The thought of the girl's slackness gave her a fleeting satisfaction. There was a light in the Habgoods' bedroom window, but she had arrived too early. Once the front door had been unlocked she could go in quietly and upstairs to the flat. The best thing would be to wait in the yard, out of the wind.

As she reached it, Evelyn was unpleasantly surprised to see a strange car parked there. Laura had said nothing about a visitor: it would make the situation even worse if one had turned up. She was staring at the car in dismay when she heard the unmistakable sound of the boiler house door banging in the wind. That it should be open at all was so incomprehensible that she forgot her immediate worries and went to investigate. Much to her relief, the boiler seemed to be functioning normally, but anyone could have got into the library, of course. She hesitated for a moment, switching on her torch. For the first time, terror gripped her.

The *trompe-l'œil* was opening very slowly...

The next moment she cursed herself for a fool. It was only the draught, of course. She grabbed the swinging panel and pushed it open, stifling a scream as the beam of light from her torch picked out old Evelyn's portrait, bringing him out of the darkness towards her...

Once more under control, she walked deliberately into the middle of the library, playing the light round the great room, to assure herself that all was well.

In due course, it rested on the huddled form of Annabel Lucas at the foot of the spiral staircase.

She was dead, her cheek marble to the touch of a finger.

Evelyn Escott reached her breaking point and fled in panic.

Chapter 3

'Soon as I saw'n I said to myself, why that's Miss Fenner's car, an' the wind's blown them yard doors open again,' Flo Dibble remarked as she took off her dripping mackintosh. 'My, did 'ee ever see a mornin' like et? 'Tis all they people flyin' about up there in the 'evins, I says. 'T'weren't never meant.'

'A real beast of a morning,' Laura Habgood agreed, avoiding controversial topics. 'Aren't your stockings wet, Flo?'

'They'm dry as a chip, thank you, Mis' Habgood, thank to me boots. I'll jest get me slippers on, and there won't be no wet on the 'all floor.'

Flo Dibble believed in keeping to your routine. As usual she started off with a vigorous attack on the cloakrooms, kitchenette and office. Next she turned her attention to the hall, and rounded off this section of her work by polishing the brass handle of the front door until it positively gleamed. The fact that it was raining did not deter her. In her view, the way you kept the brass, rain or fine, was your status symbol as a cleaner.

Now it was the turn of the library. Laura Habgood had unlocked it for her, and she headed towards the door pushing the Hoover in front of her, a diminutive figure with an habitual frown etched between her eyebrows and stray wisps of home-bobbed hair sticking out at odd angles.

Her reaction on entering the room was that the central heating must have gone wrong. It felt quite chilly instead of nice and warm as usual. She looked up at the fanlights of the cupolas, expecting to see that a pane of glass had been blown in by the gale, as had happened once before, but there was no sign of any damage. As her gaze returned to ground level it came to rest at the foot of the spiral staircase.

Several seconds elapsed during which Flo stood stock still. Then suddenly she began to scream, shrilly and continuously, unconsciously releasing the pent-up tensions of years.

The horrifying sound penetrated to the kitchen of the flat, where the Habgoods were at breakfast with Alastair's niece, Clare Fenner. Laura dropped her knife with a clatter and dashed to the door leading into the gallery, with Clare close behind and Alastair following as fast as his limp allowed. One look at Flo Dibble standing in the middle of the library floor sent Laura running to the spiral staircase. She was on it before she saw the body below.

'Alastair!' she gasped. 'Annabel's fallen right down.'

Before Clare could join her she was on her knees below, looking up at her husband, with an ashen face.

'I think she's dead. She's quite cold.'

'Dr Masterman,' he said. 'If he's out, 999.'

Laura scrambled to her feet and ran down the library. As she passed, Flo Dibble stopped screaming with the suddenness of a radio being switched off. Clare Fenner, poised halfway down the staircase, and feeling marooned between heaven and earth in the startling silence, manoeuvred herself round and rejoined her uncle in the gallery.

'It's your assistant, isn't it?' she said. 'How absolutely ghastly if she's been lying there all night. Was she working late, or something?'

'I simply can't understand it,' he said, looking appalled and completely bewildered. 'She came up with my letters just before she went off last night, and there was no question of her staying on for anything.'

'I suppose she must have come back to fetch something from the gallery. Do you think?–'

Clare broke off, realizing he was not listening. He was staring, aghast, at the section of the gallery that ran across the back of the hall.

'Good God! Look over there – that's the cupboard where we keep the valuable books…'

In her turn, Clare stared at its forced lock and gaping doors. Alastair Habgood took a few steps towards it, but abruptly checked himself.

'Leave everything as it is for the police, I suppose … I'll go and ring them. Clare, do you think you could stay up here for a minute or two? I think we perhaps oughtn't just to clear out altogether, as things are.'

'Of course I can,' she assured him. 'I don't mind a bit.'

When he had disappeared into the flat she took a step back from the balustrade, and leaned against the bookshelves, surprised and slightly ashamed at her feeling of discomfort. After all, people died in accidents every day. She shut her eyes and tried to analyse her feelings more exactly. Could it be some atavistic tabu about dead bodies popping up? Surely not, in this day and age, when one was twenty-five, and had been holding down a responsible job for years? Clare opened her eyes again, steady blue-grey ones in an attractive, rounded face with a light sprinkle of freckles, and contemplated the broken doors of the cupboard. Wasn't there something very odd about this whole situation? If you worked in a library it must be fairly simple to pinch books. Breaking in during the night didn't ring true, somehow. Suppose the girl had come back to fetch something, and surprised the real thief ... and been chucked down the staircase? Murdered, to call things by their names?

The effect of this reconstruction was to make Clare unconsciously edge away in the direction of the flat. As she did so, Laura Habgood opened the library door.

'Dr Masterman's on his way,' she said. 'Come down and wait here, Clare. I'm just coping with Flo. Where's Alastair?'

'Ringing the police. The cupboard where the valuable books are kept has been smashed open.'

Laura vanished with a horrified exclamation.

Dr Masterman, the Habgoods' GP, and Detective-Inspector Cook of the Ramsden CID stood looking down at Annabel Lucas's body.

'Fractured her skull in falling, from the look of it,' the former said. 'Twelve hours ago, at a rough guess.'

Inspector Cook grunted. 'I'd better ring for the usual support, I suppose. There was a phone in that office place, wasn't there?'

The call made, he sat on for a few moments, frowning. A combined accidental death and robbery in a rum set-up like this looked like a lot of work. He wished he had joined the Ramsden Literary and Scientific and been along to some gardening talks. People said they were quite good; and he would have got the hang of the building. Visited by an idea he returned to Dr Masterman in the library.

'You a member of this outfit, Doc?' he asked.

'Yes. Why?'

'You might put me in the picture, then. I've never been inside the door till now.'

Dr Masterman obliged with a succinct account of the function, layout and current employees of the Athenaeum.

'Thanks, that's better. So, if she didn't hide up in here at closing time last night, she must either have slipped through the flat upstairs or got hold of a key, either to the library door or to the one behind those fake bookshelves.'

'That's the boiler house door, and Habgood says it's bolted on the inside as well as being kept locked.'

Inspector Cook advanced upon the *trompe-l'œil* and looked at it disapprovingly. Fancy touches in a case were the end, he thought.

'Hang on a minute, Doc, will you?' he said. 'I'll just go round and give the outside of that door the once over.'

Regardless of the rain, which was still quite heavy, he subjected the yard to close scrutiny. It ran the full length of the Athenaeum and was only overlooked by the side windows of the flat. At the far end and on the side opposite these windows it was surrounded by a high brick wall. It was clear that the only access was through the double doors and by way of the boiler house. Inspector Cook briefly inspected the prefabricated garage which housed the Habgoods' Austin 1100, and the Mini parked in the open, but found nothing of interest. The contents of the two dustbins were equally unhelpful. A keen gardener, he glanced disapprovingly at the cat ladder from the bathroom window, then ran hurriedly down the yard to the door of the boiler house. Having satisfied himself that the rain would long ago have washed off any prints, he opened the door without difficulty and peered inside.

Of course she'd have had to get hold of the key, he thought. Easy enough to slip back the bolt some time on Wednesday when she was working in the library...

He shut the door again, and retraced his steps, slamming the double doors behind him and testing them to make sure that the Yale lock held. As he did so, two cars containing his support drew up.

Events began to move fast. Dr Masterman conferred with the police surgeon and departed. Annabel Lucas's body was photographed from numerous angles, then removed to a waiting mortuary van. The police surgeon left to arrange for a postmortem. Inspector Cook briefed his technicians, instructing them to concentrate in the first instance on the boiler house, the book cupboard and the spiral staircase. He then sent a polite message to the Habgoods to the effect that he would be glad to see them both in the office.

They impressed him favourably. Although obviously shaken, they gave him all the information he asked for, clearly and concisely. He learned that Annabel Lucas and her husband had come to Ramsden about two years ago, and opened a small antique shop.

'In Moneypenny Street,' Laura told him. 'It's more of a good class junk shop, really.'

Inspector Cook, who knew his Ramsden, placed it at once and nodded.

It appeared that the couple had parted company and that Annabel had continued to run the shop, taking part-time jobs in the afternoons. She had been working as librarian's assistant at the Athenaeum for over a year. The Habgoods did not know if there had been a separation or a divorce.

'She was cagey about her past history,' Alastair said. 'On the defensive, we always thought. One gathered that she felt she'd been badly let down by the husband.'

'If there was no legal arrangement, he's her next of kin,' Inspector Cook commented. 'We'll have to get on to it at once. I'll ring the station and have someone sent round to the shop to look for any letters or addresses.'

This done, he began to ask the Habgoods about the previous evening.

'So you didn't actually see Mrs Lucas leave the premises, then?' he asked Laura.

'No. I ran upstairs to answer the telephone, and when I came down she had gone – or so I thought. But one of the members was leaving at the same moment, so she might be able to tell you. A Miss Escott: we can look up her address for you in the membership file.'

'Wait a bit ... Escott, did you say? A lady of that name was knocked down and had her handbag snatched yesterday evening. Funny coincidence, if it's the same one.'

'One, Alma Cottages, Alexandra Road,' Alastair told him, looking up from a card index file.

'That's it. I happened to be in the station when the patrol car reported.'

The Habgoods exclaimed in dismay.

'I must ring her and ask how she is,' Laura said. 'What a wretched thing to happen.'

'Not just for the next hour or two, please, Mrs Habgood. I'd rather she heard about Mrs Lucas's accident from me. Now, I'd like to know a bit more about your security arrangements here. I understand the door from the hall into the library is locked when you close at half-past five, and not opened again until the cleaning woman comes at half-past seven next morning? Right? What about the way through from the boiler house?'

'The boiler house door into the yard is permanently locked, except when the boiler's being serviced, and it's bolted on the inside as well.'

'Then how do you account for the fact that we found it unlocked and unbolted this morning?'

Inspector Cook watched the Habgoods closely as he asked this question. They stared at him in blank astonishment, Laura stifling an exclamation of amazement.

'I can't account for it. It's quite incomprehensible,' Alastair said. 'To the best of my knowledge it hasn't been opened since September. We always have the boiler serviced then, before the central heating season starts.'

'Who would be responsible for locking up after the servicing?'

'I am,' Laura said. 'And I remember perfectly well doing it. The bolt seemed to have got a bit stiff and I had to work it along.'

'Where are the keys of these doors kept?' Inspector Cook asked abruptly.'

'On a board in our bedroom with all the other house keys,' Alastair replied, looking worried. 'That's been the arrangement ever since we came here. I suggested it myself to the House Committee and they approved.'

Feeling that his inquiries were shaping nicely, and pointing to the obvious conclusion about Annabel Lucas's presence in the library, Inspector Cook asked about the door from the gallery into the Habgoods' flat. At this point it struck him that they were reacting rather differently, Alastair appearing decidedly unhappy, while his wife seemed to be taking the bit between her teeth.

'Let's face it,' she said categorically. 'We *do* forget to lock it, sometimes, when we're both going to be out of the flat. We did on your free afternoon last week. I remember saying that, since there have been so many robberies in the town, we really ought to be more careful. Anyone could walk straight in from the library.'

There was a pause.

'Let's face something else,' suggested Inspector Cook. 'Have you ever both been out of the building altogether while Mrs Lucas was on duty in the library?'

'Yes,' Laura replied briefly. 'Last week, for instance.'

Alastair moved uneasily in his chair.

'I must come in here, Inspector. Mrs Lucas is dead and can't defend herself. I can only say that I've never questioned her honesty. Besides, other people are around when we have functions. Last Tuesday night at the centenary party the flat was open for anybody who wanted to look at the ceilings.'

Laura's quick glance at her husband made Inspector Cook wonder briefly if it could have been the old story of the wife and the secretary. Unlikely, he thought, glancing in turn at Alastair. But would a scholar chap like him have been up to fiddles and whatever?

He inquired further into arrangements for access to the flat during the centenary party.

'Can't say I'd relish strangers wandering around my place,' he commented. 'Ever had anything pinched?'

'Never,' Alastair replied. 'It isn't exactly a case of strangers, you know. They'd all be RLSS members and their guests. Anyway, we lock up our modest valuables and any cash, just as a precaution.'

Inspector Cook considered. 'Would you have noticed if the boiler house key had been "borrowed", shall we call it, at any time? Say last Tuesday night?'

Both Habgoods were emphatic that they would. 'I was last in on Tuesday night,' Alastair told him. 'I locked the front door and took the key upstairs. I'm positive that I should have noticed if the boiler house key hadn't been on the board. The front door key hangs next to it.'

'And I should have noticed when I took the front door key down on Wednesday morning, when I let the cleaner in,' added Laura.

'Fair enough,' Inspector Cook agreed. 'Well, we've covered some useful ground, and thank you both for your help. We'll have to keep the place closed until we've finished going over the library, I'm afraid. Let me see, it's Mr Westlake who's head of things here, isn't it?'

'Yes, he's my Chairman,' Alastair replied. 'He's gone to London for the day, unfortunately, and I can't get at him.'

'If the woman who found the body's calmed down, I'd better have a word with her before she goes home.'

'She's up in the flat having cups of tea,' Laura said. 'Shall I fetch her?'

'I'll come up, if it's convenient, and take a look at the gallery door and the board for the keys.'

He saw that the flat was shut off by a door

at the top of the staircase, which had a Chubb lock.

'We remember to lock this one if the flat is going to be empty,' Alastair said, reading his thoughts. 'It's our private front door. Not the sort of thing one overlooks, like the gallery door. The key board's in here. You can't see it behind the door and we prop all the doors wide open when people are coming round.'

Having satisfied himself on this point, Inspector Cook borrowed the boiler house key to be tested for traces of an impression having been taken, and had a brief interview with a subdued Flo Dibble. He then went downstairs, reasonably satisfied with his progress to date.

Lucas, all right, he thought. Easy as pie for her to get at the boiler house key. She could have taken an impression and got a duplicate cut earlier on, or unlocked the door days ago: the chances were a hundred to one against anyone spotting it. And she could have slipped back the bolt any time on Wednesday when nobody was in the library... All this laid on to cover up pinching books. Suppose she thought nobody would connect the theft with her, seeing she could help herself at any time... The job now is finding out what made her pitch down that spiral staircase contraption...

He went into the library. Detective-Constable Neale, a keen young fingerprint expert, was examining the spiral staircase with the aid of a powerful electric lamp. He hastily descended the pair of steps strategically placed beside it, and hurried forward with the expression of a fox terrier on a promising scent.

'Quite a party in here last night, sir,' he said enthusiastically. 'Three lots of dabs on the inside handle of the boiler house door. One lot under deceased's, and one on top.'

Inspector Cook had the sensation of being pulled up with a sharp and unexpected jerk.

'The bottom lot'll be Mrs Habgood's,' he said prosaically. 'She says she shut the place up after the boiler was serviced.'

Constable Neale's expression changed to that of a conjuror about to produce a rabbit from a hat.

'I wouldn't know about that, sir, but they're the same ones that are on the cupboard. Chap wearing rubber gloves, I'd say. Deceased's aren't on the cupboard at all. Only on some of the books tumbled out of it, as if she'd looked 'em over.'

Inspector Cook did not reply immediately,

his mind being occupied with the door from the flat on to the gallery, and the change in Laura Habgood's attitude that had struck him.

'What about the top lot of dabs?' he asked, returning to the immediate present.

'Gloved ones again, sir. Knitted ones, from the look of 'em, and smudged, as if they were damp. Wet patches on the boiler house floor, too, and a pool o' water, as if an umbrella'd been stood up against the wall.'

Without comment, Inspector Cook strode towards the *trompe-l'œil*.

Half an hour later he left the Athenaeum, gloomily recognizing the fact that the circumstances of Annabel Lucas's death were going to take the hell of a lot of investigating.

'One, Alma Cottages, Alexandra Road,' he told his driver, after consulting his notebook, deciding to get this loose end tidied up before returning to report to his Superintendent.

The woman who opened the door to him went so white that he thought that she was going to faint.

'Miss Escott, madam? I'm sorry if I startled you. It's Inspector Cook. I'm afraid I haven't come with any news of your handbag yet, but to ask if you can give me a bit of help over an inquiry I'm making.'

Expectancy drained out of her face. He thought that she looked apprehensive.

'Won't you come in?' she said almost inaudibly.

He followed her into a diminutive sitting room, and took the chair she indicated.

'I won't keep you more than a minute or two,' he told her, trying to sound friendly and encouraging. 'I'd like you to cast your mind back to yesterday evening, round about half-past five. I understand you were leaving the Athenaeum in Abbot's Green at that time. Right?'

She nodded without speaking.

'Were you alone?'

'No.' She hesitated a moment, then went on, 'I left with the librarian's assistant, Mrs Lucas.'

'Did you go far together?'

'Oh, no. She went to get her car. I haven't one.'

'Did you notice if she went back into the building?'

'I'm quite sure she didn't. I heard her drive away towards the town.'

'And you didn't see her again yesterday evening?'

'No. I came straight home, here.'

'And on the way you had that nasty experience of being knocked down and having your bag snatched,' Inspector Cook said sympathetically. 'I'm afraid I've got some unpleasant news for you, too.'

As he told her that Annabel Lucas's body had been found in the library, she slipped quietly to the floor, in the faint that he had half expected when he arrived.

Delayed shock, I suppose, he thought, administering first aid.

To his relief, Evelyn Escott came round quickly. 'I'm sorry I was so stupid,' she apologized tremulously. 'I didn't sleep very well last night.'

'Not to be wondered at,' he replied. 'And now this is another shock on top of the first one, but you were bound to hear about Mrs Lucas sooner or later, weren't you? Now, when you parted last night, did you notice anything unusual about her? Did she seemed worried or excited, for instance?'

Evelyn Escott shook her head. 'But I didn't know her at all well,' she said. 'It was just chance that we left the Athenaeum together.'

'In that case I needn't bother you any more,' he said. 'It's possible you may be wanted at the inquest, but don't worry about that now. I'd take the day quietly if I were you, Miss Escott.'

Shortly afterwards he left for his headquarters, dismissing her from his mind as he assembled facts for his report to Superintendent Daly. It took some time to deliver it, and the two men decided that little further progress could be made until more information had come in.

'The P-M report won't be ready till late this afternoon,' Superintendent Daly said, 'and we'll be darned lucky if we get anything on the dabs from the Yard by then. Meanwhile, Mills is round at the shop, trying to pick up what he can, and I suppose Neale may get something from the staircase. Say nine o'clock tonight then. I'll get on to the CC right away.'

The news that there had been a fatal accident at the Athenaeum leaked out in the course of the morning. On emerging from Superintendent Daly's room, Inspector Cook learned that a reporter from the *Ramsden Recorder* was waiting to see him. With some skill, he managed to imply indirectly that there was nothing unusual in Annabel Lucas's working late in the library, nor in the fact that her body had not been found until the next morning, owing to the disruption caused by Alastair Habgood's being out of action. He decided to make no reference at the moment to the stolen books and the mystery of the unlocked and unbolted boiler house door.

Members of the Ramsden Literary and Scientific Society who found themselves being turned away from the Athenaeum by the police constable on duty were less easily fobbed off. Their familiarity with the library routine led to mounting speculation, which spread like wildfire. After several telephone calls, Alastair Habgood decided that the correct course of action in the absence of the Chairman would be to inform the other Trustees of what had happened. He rang Colin Escott at his office, only to learn that he was out inspecting a country property, was lunching at home, and was not expected to come in until two o'clock. Accordingly, at quarter to one Alastair rang the Escott home. Daphne Escott answered the telephone.

'Mr Habgood?' she queried, sounding baffled. 'My husband's not in yet. I could ask him to ring you when he's had some lunch.'

'It's an urgent matter, Mrs Escott,' Alastair replied, suppressing his nervous impatience. 'Will you ask him to ring as soon

81

as he comes in, please?'

Daphne began to make difficulties but broke off suddenly to say that she could hear the car coming in. 'You'd better hold on,' she said ungraciously.

Half a minute later, after a distinct acrimonious-sounding exchange, there were footsteps and the receiver was picked up.

'Escott here,' came Colin's loud voice. 'What's up?'

'Something serious, I'm afraid, Mr Escott,' Alastair replied. 'Mrs Lucas, my assistant, was found with a fractured skull at the bottom of the spiral staircase this morning. The cleaner discovered her soon after eight.'

'Good God! Why are you ringing me, though? Westlake's the Chairman.'

'Mr Westlake went to London by the first train this morning and it's impossible to contact him.'

Colin Escott swore fluently.

'Whatever medico you sent for called the police in, I suppose?'

'Yes. Inspector Cook is now in charge. Unfortunately, that isn't all. The accident happened last night, according to medical evidence, after the library had closed and Mrs Lucas had officially left. It's not clear how she returned. And the cupboard where we keep valuable books has been broken open – about half a dozen are missing.'

'Woman was a crook, from the look of it. I suppose we're covered by our insurance?'

'Our own books are. I'm not sure about one which was on loan from Mr Westlake.'

'Well, if he isn't covered by his own policy, that's his funeral, not ours … of course, I'm sorry you're having all this bother, Habgood, but there's nothing I can do now that the police have moved in. Just land the ball in Westlake's court as soon as he gets back. Thanks for ringing.'

Striding into the kitchen, Colin gave Daphne the gist of the conversation. She paused in the act of taking a casserole out of the oven, and stared at him.

'What an extraordinary thing to happen,' she commented with faint surprise. 'Do go and wash, Colin, and come and have your lunch. I'm afraid it may be a bit overdone.'

Later, in the course of the meal, Colin gave a sudden guffaw.

'What price Evelyn's history of RLSS now?' he said. 'This ought to liven it up a bit!… Hell! Some sort of gesture's called for, I suppose. Ask the Habgoods over, what?'

Peter Escott seldom went home to lunch,

much preferring to make do with a snack in a congenial bar. On this occasion he patronized the Abbot's Buttery in the semi-basement of Ramsden's leading hotel. The management had attempted to create a mediaeval atmosphere by means of bogus oak beams, rough wooden benches and tables and dim lighting. The room was packed with lunchtime drinkers, and as Peter elbowed his way forward he caught the word 'Athenaeum' above the deafening conversations in progress.

'Yes, old Buckmaster,' a man just in front of him was shouting. 'Met him in the post office just now. He'd been round to look something up in the library, and found the place closed and the police in possession. All he could get out of 'em was that there'd been a fatal accident last night, and nobody was being let in until further notice...'

'The usual, sir?'

Peter Escott surfaced abruptly, surprised to find that he had arrived at the bar. 'I'll have a double whisky today, George,' he said.

Unable to escape being drawn into a group of friends, he ate and drank hurriedly, announcing that he had got to meet a client during the lunch hour. Outside the hotel he stood on the pavement for a few moments debating with himself, and finally started off in the direction of Abbot's Green.

As he approached the Athenaeum the front door opened and was closed again by someone inside as a girl came out, carrying a shopping bag. Peter Escott made a split-second decision.

'Excuse me,' he said. 'No, I'm not a reporter. I've just heard that there's been a serious accident here, and thought I'd come along and try to find out what's happened. I'm Peter Escott: my people have been mixed up with this place for ages. I know Mr and Mrs Habgood,' he added, with a note of inquiry, registering that the girl was a serious type but easy on the eye.

Clare Fenner hesitated briefly, torn between an impulse to respond emotionally to what seemed to be a kind gesture, and her natural circumspection, enhanced by professional training as a confidential secretary. How much were the police saying, she wondered?

'How nice of you to come round,' she said. 'I'm Clare Fenner, a niece. No, it isn't my uncle and aunt, thank goodness. It's my uncle's assistant, a Mrs Lucas. She seems to have fallen down the spiral staircase in the library last night. The cleaner found her this morning – dead. And there seems some mystery about why she was there at all. It's all absolutely beastly for Uncle Alastair and Aunt Laura. I'd just come for last night on my way down to my people in Devon, but I'm staying on to try and give a spot of moral support... I don't think they much want callers at the moment, to be honest.'

Meeting her clear gaze, Peter Escott hastily expressed sympathy, which she promised to pass on to the Habgoods. He hesitated.

'Are you going into town?' he asked tentatively. 'I'm on my way to the office. May I come along?'

'Yes, do,' Clare replied. 'I thought it might be a good time to collect up some food. I don't want to be out long.'

'Lucky for the Habgoods you happened to be around,' Peter said, as they walked along. 'I suppose the place mayn't be able to open again for days if the police are trying to find out what happened?'

Clare, on the brink of telling him about the book theft, came down at the last moment on the side of reticence.

'I suppose not,' she said. 'I don't think anyone has a clue at the moment.'

Realizing that no further information was

forthcoming, Peter began to make polite inquiries about her home and job. To his surprise he found himself diverging from his route to escort her to the shopping centre.

'Thanks most awfully,' she said, rather distractedly, as he pointed out the greengrocer patronized by his mother. 'You've been so kind... Good-bye.'

He watched her disappear into the shop, and began to retrace his steps. Back in his room at Escott House, where the family firm had its head office, he was sitting at his desk doing nothing in particular when the door opened and his father came in.

'You're back from lunch very early,' Colin remarked. 'Congratulations. I suppose you've heard about this business at the Athenaeum? It seems to be all over the town. Habgood's assistant was picked up dead at the bottom of the spiral staircase this morning, and a bunch of valuable books is missing. Looks as though the woman was involved, doesn't it?'

'What do the police think?' Peter asked.

'God, I don't know. Haven't asked 'em. The more we keep out of it the better. Unfortunately Westlake's in town till tonight. Bit of a comedown after all the tripe he talked on Tuesday... Has that chap after the house in Mortlake Avenue made a firm offer?'

87

'I daresay my butting in like this is a bit unorthodox,' James Westlake said, 'but dammit, I'm Chairman of RLSS, and a JP too, if that's relevant.'

'Entirely irrelevant,' replied the Chief Constable, an old friend. 'But as we're just arriving at the moment of truth, you can attend as an observer if Daly doesn't mind.'

Superintendent Daly, who had a high opinion of James Westlake's performance on the Bench, said that it was OK by him.

'Right. Light up and listen, then, James. When you barged in we were considering whether or not to call in the Yard.'

James Westlake stopped dead in the act of extracting a tobacco pouch from his coat pocket, and looked his astonishment.

'As you've just come from the Athenaeum, I take it that you know as much as the Habgoods do,' the Chief Constable went on, 'but quite a bit's transpired since this morning. There's a good deal more to this business than Mrs Lucas's accidental death while apparently helping herself to books. Whether they were her accomplices or not we don't yet know, but two other people were illicitly in the library in the course of last night. Call them X and Y. X came in before Lucas, and did the breaking open of the cupboard. He wore rubber gloves. *Y* came after Lucas, and was wearing knitted gloves. The dabs suggest that she was a woman. Lucas has a record. She was twice convicted of shop-lifting from London stores some years ago, and once of receiving stolen property.'

James Westlake looked appalled.

'We took up one of her references when she applied for the job at the Athenaeum, of course. It was satisfactory.'

'With the shortage of typists, she probably had no difficulty in getting jobs between whiles. Coming now to a more serious aspect of this business, it's not at all clear why she pitched down a staircase that she was quite familiar with in her daily work. We've made a preliminary examination, but there doesn't seem to be any structural defect, and there are no traces of mud or anything slippery on the treads or the soles of the shoes she was wearing. We got up some dust and whatever with the suction gadget and have sent it off to the Forensic Lab for tests, but it's difficult to see that it's going to help much, if at all. Finally, the P-M report says there's no sign of her having been given a hefty shove from behind. On the other hand, they point out that it wouldn't take much of a push, on a contraption like that staircase, to make her slip – especially if she was carrying books and hurrying. Well, that's the gist of it. What's your conclusion about bringing in the Yard, Daly?'

Superintendent Daly slumped back in his chair, frowning. 'I'm not saying we couldn't handle the inquiry, sir. But Inspector Cook and I've been talking it over and we think the roots of it all are in London, not Ramsden. She must have been in with a shady lot up there, at one time. With her husband going off, she may have linked up with 'em again. The Yard's better placed than we are to follow these people up, and then there's tracing the books that were taken. We both feel it's a Yard job.'

The Chief Constable looked at James Westlake. 'What's your reaction? It'll mean a lot of publicity, of course.'

'I don't care a damn about publicity, provided we can get the whole thing cleared up as quickly as possible. It's bloody unpleasant for RLSS, and especially for the Habgoods. I'm all for the Yard, for the Super's reasons. Let's hope they send us someone good.'

'I've got a bit of leverage with one of the Assistant Commissioners,' the Chief Constable said meditatively. 'I'll ring his private number on chance.'

'Old School Tie?'

'No. Arms, companions in. I hoicked him out of the sea at Dunkirk.'

'Should help,' James Westlake agreed.

'Sorry one of your books was taken, sir,' Superintendent Daly said to James, when the Chief Constable had gone to put through his call. 'Something pretty valuable, wasn't it?'

'Best thing I've got, unfortunately. It was on loan for the exhibition we had at the centenary party on Tuesday night. An illustrated study of the county in the author's handwriting. Eighteenth century.'

The two policemen commiserated.

'Mightn't its being on show at the party be a lead?' Inspector Cook said suddenly.

'I suppose it's possible. There were over 130 people there, though.'

The return of the Chief Constable broke off the discussion.

'It did help, actually,' he remarked. 'We're getting that Pollard bloke.'

Superintendent Daly and Inspector Cook both whistled.

Chapter 4

Friday afternoon was wan and still, made eerie by wreathing wisps of fog. The library at the Athenaeum blazed with electric light but remained dead. Withered flowers and leaves stood gauntly in vases. Surfaces were filmed with dust, and tables and chairs jostled in confusion.

Detective-Superintendent Tom Pollard stood in front of the librarian's table with an impassive expression, looking down at Detective-Sergeant Strickland stretched out on the floor. Strickland, the team's finger-print expert, was directing the beams of a powerful lamp on to a series of faint lines and depressions in the pile of the carpet. A few feet away Detective-Inspector Toye sat back on his haunches, thoughtfully contemplating the two men through his massive horn-rims.

'Seemed to us, sir, somebody'd been crawling around on all fours,' Strickland said. 'That way you drag your toes along each time you go forward, and if the pile's

93

deep it'll leave a track. Then, when you stop, there'll be a little pit where the toecap rests. Boyce tried it out over there. Have another go, Boyce.'

Detective-Sergeant Boyce, photographer, crawled a few yards on his hands and knees as requested.

Still uncharacteristically silent, Pollard dropped to the floor and inspected both sets of marks. 'Looks like it,' he said briefly, getting up again. 'May not be anything in it for us, though. Mrs Lucas could have dropped something, then gone down to hunt for it, when she was working here on Wednesday.'

'There's bits of gravel in one or two of these marks,' Toye's voice came from under the table, where he was peering at the carpet through a lens. He lowered his head still further and sniffed. 'Oil,' he said succinctly.

Pollard's head went up, an infallible sign of alerted interest. The two technicians exchanged a quick glance.

'Odd,' he said. 'Coming in from the street you don't have to pass the oil storage tank in the yard. It's several feet beyond the boiler house door. Let's have a look at the thing.'

He set off towards the *trompe-l'œil*, followed by the others.

'Hooked on the job at last,' Boyce breathed in Strickland's ear as they brought up the rear. 'What's been biting him?'

It was a five hundred gallon tank, raised from the ground on low pillars, painted green and covered by a perspex roof. Toye expressed approval.

'Save a lot of repainting. I've roofed mine,' he added with a touch of complacency.

'This roof's saved more than repainting,' Pollard said as he straightened up. 'Look here. Somebody's been standing close up to the tank on the side furthest from the road, and the roof's kept the rain off the marks.'

He shone his torch on to two depressions in the gravel, and stepped back to look down the yard towards the double doors. 'Anybody right up against the tank wouldn't be seen by somebody else coming in and making for the boiler house,' he went on, and stooped again, this time to sniff the far side of the tank and rub it with his finger. 'Definitely oily. No sign of rust or seepage, so the chap who did the last fill up must have sloshed some oil over. We'd better investigate Mrs Lucas's coat and shoes if they're back from the lab. Nip round to the station, Toye, and bring 'em along. We'll collect gravel samples from both places while you're gone.'

While Boyce and Strickland began this operation, Pollard returned to the library. He flung himself into a leather armchair, crossed his legs and clasped his hands behind his head. After considerable initial disgruntlement he was feeling a first stirring of interest in the inquiry. He had resented having it foisted upon him, partly because a postponement of leave was involved and partly because he suspected what he called Old School Tie wire-pulling. The AC had been too elaborately casual about knowing the Chief Constable. In addition, the job looked open and shut. A woman with a record and shady acquaintances plans a book theft, involving her former mates to divert suspicion from herself as an employee, falls down a lethal spiral staircase and expires. Exeunt shady acquaintances with booty, leaving a corpse with no marks of violence. Just a tedious tracking-down of the chaps and the books, and precious little kudos, even if one caught up with 'em.

Pollard suddenly grinned, remembering an astringent remark by his wife, Jane, to the effect that he'd better watch out or his spiritual home would soon be the headlines. Anyway, the present situation had just sprouted a curious thought-provoking feature. He had been exhaustively briefed by Inspector Cook after the adjourned inquest, and was quite clear about the sets of fingerprints on the inside handle of the boiler house door. *X* had come in first and subsequently broken open the cupboard containing the library's more valuable books. Lucas had come in next, after hiding behind the oil tank in the yard. She had inexplicably crawled about on the floor under the librarian's table, then gone up to the gallery. Here she had examined the books lying scattered in front of the cupboard, and collected up the first editions of the Palliser novels. Subsequently, and for no reason established as yet, she had fallen down the spiral staircase, dropping the books and her torch, and fatally fracturing her skull. Last of all, *Y* had come, adding the bizarre touch of wet knitted gloves and a dripping umbrella to the curious sequence of events. Much later than *X* and Lucas, presumably, as the heavy rain had not started until midnight.

Pollard absently watched Strickland collecting fragments of gravel from the carpet with forceps and dropping them into a sterilized container. Why on earth, if Lucas and *X* were on the job together, and she had opened up the boiler house door for it, had she hidden outside on a cold November evening instead of waiting for him inside? Could the robbery have been entirely *X's* affair, and Lucas have chanced on it, waiting behind the tank to identify him as he came out? No, that wouldn't wash, of course. Even assuming that she had come back to fetch something on Wednesday evening, she couldn't have expected to get into the library through the boiler house, even if the yard doors were open. She would have rung the front door bell and asked to be let through. And, of course, *X* would somehow have had to unbolt the boiler house door. He couldn't have known that the gates were going to be reopened for the librarian's niece…

At this juncture Toye reappeared, carrying two plastic bags.

Inspection of Annabel Lucas's coat at once established the fact that its wearer had recently leaned against an oily surface. Her shoes were the fashionable platform type, black patent with a T-strap across the instep. Scrapings had been taken from the shoes and heels for forensic tests. The Yard men contemplated the pair in silence.

'If they passed a law that women had got

to wear things like this, there'd be demos and riots,' Toye commented.

Pollard snatched up the shoes and inspected them closely. 'Don't knock the rag trade chap who dreamed up this pair. See here.'

He pointed to the motif of small rectangular depressions that ran round the exposed edge of the sole, several of which contained fragments of gravel, and sniffed vigorously once more. 'Oily,' he said triumphantly. 'Dig the gravel out, Strickland, for a third sample. Toye, I think we'd–'

He broke off. From beyond the hall came the perennially sinister sound of someone walking purposefully but unrhythmically with a stick. A loud rap on the library door followed.

'Oo-er!' remarked Detective-Sergeant Boyce, an irrepressible extrovert.

'Come in!' Pollard called, drowning Toye's scandalized rebuke.

The man who entered, limping slightly, was of medium height and build, and pale and scholarly in appearance. He wore spectacles, and his thinning hair was receding from his temples.

'Alastair Habgood,' he said. 'I'm librarian here. This mayn't be according to the book, but my wife would be glad to send down some tea if you'd care for it.'

'That's awfully good of her,' Pollard replied. 'I must say we'd be glad of a cuppa. As a matter of fact, I was just coming to ask if you could spare us a few minutes.'

'Supposing you come up and have one with us, then? We're just starting tea, and can send some down here for your colleagues.'

With tactful slowness Pollard and Toye followed Alastair Habgood upstairs. As they passed through the door at the top, the oppressive deadness of the ground floor was replaced by cosy domesticity. There was a welcoming smell of toasted buns. They crossed a small landing, Pollard's quick eye for the layout of the building enabling him to locate the door on to the gallery, deeply recessed in a thick wall. Two women sitting by a tea trolley looked up with interest as they came in.

'I've brought along Superintendent Pollard and Inspector Toye for a working tea, dear,' Alastair Habgood told his wife.

In the small bustle of introductions and the bringing up of extra chairs, Clare Fenner undertook to take a tray down to the library, and went out. Pollard looked about him, and tilted his head back.

'What a marvellous room,' he said. 'I suppose this is the oldest part of the building?'

The Habgoods reacted with pleased surprise, and for a short time the conversation was historical and architectural. As they talked, it struck Pollard that Laura Habgood was a very different type from her husband. A cheerful, practical sort, he thought, studying her broad animated face, lively dark eyes and springy hair. Decided, too, with that strong chin. He remembered that according to Cook's report in the case file she had had little use for Annabel Lucas, and felt no doubt at all that the girl had been responsible for the break-in.

'Well,' he said, when a pause developed, 'I'm afraid I must bother you with a lot of questions, most of which you'll have answered already. We Yard chaps do like to get our facts at first-hand. How about Miss Fenner? She was here on Wednesday night, wasn't she?'

'Yes, she was,' Laura replied. 'All right, Alastair, I'll get her.' Forestalling her husband, she was at the door before he could get out of his chair.

Clare Fenner reappeared and slipped into a chair next to Toye, who smiled at her encouragingly.

'Were you surprised,' Pollard asked without preamble, 'when you heard that your Chief Constable had called in the Yard?'

Both Habgoods nodded affirmatively.

'Very much so,' Alastair replied. 'It's a wretched business with a tragic ending, but hardly complicated, I should have thought.'

'It's time now, I think,' Pollard said, 'that you were put more fully into the picture. As well as Mrs Lucas, there were two other unauthorized people in your library during Friday night.'

He watched momentary incredulity give way to horrified dismay in their faces. He also thought that there had been a fleeting glimpse of something very like relief in Laura's.

'It's absolutely appalling to think of all this going on under our own roof!' Alastair exclaimed. 'I can only say I'm thankful Scotland Yard *has* been called in.'

'You've both made very full and helpful statements to Inspector Cook,' Pollard told them, 'but there are just a few points I'd like to take a bit further. Where are the keys to the Yale lock of the yard doors kept? On the key board in your bedroom with the others?'

'One is. Mrs Lucas has the other. She parked in the yard when she was working here. We shall get it back, shan't we?'

'Of course, although probably not until the end of the inquiry. Were the doors kept locked?'

'No, not by day. The cleaner opens them in the morning to get to the dustbins. Mrs Lucas always shut them when she went in the evening, unless we told her we were taking the car out. If it wasn't one of her days here, one of us would shut them at half-past five, when the library closed.'

'I understand,' Pollard said, 'that she shut them as usual last Wednesday night, but that Mrs Habgood opened them again shortly afterwards, having just heard from Miss Fenner that she was arriving shortly by car for the night.'

'Quite correct,' Laura agreed.

'Now the point I want an opinion on is this. We know that Mrs Lucas came back here on foot. If she did this with no criminal intent, while the gates were open for Miss Fenner, would she have been so surprised that she would have gone into the yard and had a look round?'

The Habgoods looked at each other.

'I suppose she might have,' Alastair said doubtfully. 'To see if my wife had taken the car out for some reason for instance, leaving me in bed in the flat. If she had come to fetch something she'd left behind, she mightn't have wanted to ring. But I should think she could have seen at once if our garage was open and empty without going right into the yard past the boiler house door and noticing if it was open. This is what you're getting at, I take it?'

Laura Habgood had been barely concealing her impatience.

'Surely this is a bit far-fetched?' she broke in. 'I mean, if somebody else had got into the library, they'd have had to get hold of two keys, as well as managing to unbolt the boiler house door on the inside. Pretty difficult for an outsider.'

'All the same, we can't altogether rule out the possibility at the moment,' Pollard replied. 'Can we accept the fact that no one in Ramsden besides yourselves knew that Miss Fenner was coming on Wednesday evening?'

'Perhaps I'd better come in here,' Clare said. 'I didn't know myself until nearly half-past five, when my boss came in and gave me an unexpected week off while he flew out to Malta to see his new grandson. It was a bit late to get down to my parents in Devon that night, so I thought of my uncle and aunt here, as it's on the way.'

Pollard smiled at her and thought how attractively serious she looked. 'You seem to have the right sort of boss, Miss Fenner. I'm sorry you've landed up in a trouble spot, but you can start for Devon any time you like now.'

'Actually, I'm staying,' she told him. 'I might be some help when the library's opened again.'

'Which reminds me,' Pollard told Alastair, 'we'll be through by tomorrow evening, at latest. I'm afraid the place is in a bit of a mess.'

'We'll soon get it straight for reopening on Monday,' Laura said briskly. 'The sooner members can come in again, the better.'

During a short pause Toye turned over a page in his notebook.

'To move on to another topic,' Pollard resumed, 'we're naturally anxious to pinpoint the time of Mrs Lucas's death. According to the pathologist, she was killed immediately. Her fall must have been a hefty crash, and she dropped an armful of books as well. I know the back wall of this part of the house is very thick, and that you've told Inspector Cook that you heard nothing but I want you both to think yourselves back into Wednesday evening between six and eight. This period covers the pathologist's time limit. It's often surprising what one can remember without realizing it.'

There was a further pause.

'I'm afraid I'm really no go on this,' Alastair said. 'I'd had a bad day with my beastly leg, and had taken a good whack of painkillers. I took it in when my wife came and told me Clare was coming, but I dozed off again, and was only very dimly aware of domestic noises. The linen cupboard door, and my wife bustling around, and kitchen noises: clinking of plates and stirring, and the electric blender...'

'Hold it!' Pollard cut in. They stared at him. 'Those electric gadgets make a terrific row, don't they? Can you remember when you were using the blender, Mrs Habgood?'

'Heavens! Not to the minute. Just let me think.'

Laura sat for nearly half a minute with her face in her hands. Finally she said that she remembered using the blender early on, to purée some cooked vegetables for soup. Then, almost as her last job, she had used an electric beater for egg whites for a chocolate mousse. 'Say at about ten or five minutes to seven,' she concluded.

'That would tie up with my surfacing,' Alastair said, 'I think it woke me up, and then Nox – that's our cat – finished the job by landing on my chest, and you came in almost at once to ask me how I was and if I wanted any supper. We heard Clare's car arrive while we were talking.'

'It was five past seven when I got here,' Clare contributed. 'I remember looking at my watch when I pulled up.'

Pollard sensed barely suppressed questions which he had no intention of answering.

'Was Mrs Lucas a good fit here?' he asked, abruptly changing course.

'The short answer,' Alastair replied, 'is, technically, yes. Personally, not altogether.'

Conscious once again of Laura's impatient reaction, Pollard quickly asked him to elaborate.

'She could cope with the work all right. Her typing was adequate, and she had had a little experience in a commercial lending library. I can't pretend that she was a congenial colleague. For one thing, she hadn't the general education for the job, and no interest in our aims here. And some of the older members objected to her manners, and her rather free and easy way with men. I think her husband's desertion had shaken her up badly, and her principal aim in life was to acquire another man as quickly as she could.'

'Did you see much of her, Mrs Habgood?' Pollard asked Laura.

'As little as possible,' she replied tersely. 'I found her a most objectionable young woman, and quite wrong for us here. So did quite a lot of the members. They're more inclined to complain to me than to my husband.'

'I know she was far from ideal,' Alastair agreed, 'but these days you have to take what you can get. It isn't at all easy to find somebody for a boring and not particularly well paid part-time job. As it was, she had managed to find a pensioner to look after her shop when she was working here. And for all her shortcomings as a person, she was reasonably competent – and no fool.'

'Certainly she was no fool.'

Laura's tone made Pollard glance at her.

'Well,' he said, 'you have been most helpful once again, and I think we can remove ourselves now. May we just see exactly where the key board hangs?'

He satisfied himself that it was completely hidden by the door when the latter was propped wide open, as the Habgoods assured him it had been on the night of the centenary party.

'All the doors up here were, so that anybody who felt like it could wander around and look at the ceilings.'

'You wouldn't know who did come up, I suppose?'

'I'm afraid not. We were downstairs all the evening, and there was a terrific crowd. I think we could produce a list of everybody who came to the party, given time. I know the total because of the catering.'

Pollard hesitated.

'I'm afraid it means a lot of work, but we'd be glad if you'd make a start on it in case it's needed.'

On returning to the police station they were greeted by the news that an obvious lead had petered out. The Yard had located Rex Lucas in the fracture ward of a London hospital, where he had spent the past ten days recovering from injuries received in a car crash. He had made a statement, subsequently confirmed, that he had never married the dead woman, whose name was Annabel Brown. They had lived together, first in London and then in Ramsden. About eighteen months earlier he had got fed up and left her. He had heard nothing from her since, and expressed no regret at hearing of her death, adding that she had nothing to complain about. He had left her with the rest of the lease of the shop and all the stock.

'Dead end number one,' Pollard said. 'Not that I thought anything would come from that quarter.'

He sat on, frowning, for nearly a minute. Then, suddenly thrusting back his chair, he stood up.

'Come on, let's go and eat, Toye,' he said. 'Then we'll go and have a look at the shop and the girl's living quarters. And stop grinning, damn you,' he added, surprising a satisfied expression on his subordinate's face. 'All right, all right. I know I bellyached all the way down about getting the case wished on to me, and it's fifty to one that Brown fell over her own feet. All the same, I'm finding out what these odd goings-on were in aid of, headlines or not,' he concluded emphatically, and somewhat obscurely.

Toye looked puzzled, but tactfully refrained from asking for enlightenment.

Chapter 5

Later that evening, Pollard and Toye stood contemplating Moneypenny Street, a narrow one-way link between two of Ramsden's main thoroughfares. It was flanked by small shops and offices and there were few signs of a resident population.

'Part of the historic centre, as they call the middles of towns these days,' Toye observed. 'The property developers would have flattened it, else.'

Pollard reluctantly diverted his gaze from gabled roofs and round-headed windows, and agreed.

'This looks like it,' he said, halting in front of a shop window crowded with an astonishing variety of objects, and surmounted by a lettered board proclaiming 'You Want it: We've Got it'.

Toye unlocked the door and played the beam of his torch on the walls to locate a light switch, and strip lighting stuttered into being overhead. Apart from a narrow central gangway and a space at the back, the shop was crammed with small articles of furniture and general miscellanea, all set out in orderly fashion.

'First time I've seen a junk shop lined up like this,' Toye said, trying out a rocking chair after removing a stack of suitcases from its seat. 'I've always fancied one of these...'

'Think I've brought you on a shopping expedition?' As he spoke, glancing up from a notebook labelled 'Sales', Pollard was suddenly conscious of being watched, and turned abruptly to face the street. Two faces, distorted by avid curiosity, were flattened against the glass. 'Let's get upstairs and switch this light off. Half Ramsden will be outside, soon, if we don't.'

A short flight of stairs covered with worn linoleum led up to a single large room over the shop, and a minute, scruffy bathroom, built out over the downstairs lavatory. Toye drew a curtain across the window overlooking the street. Bare boards, wallpaper faded to an indistinguishable dun colour and sparse furniture all added up to drabness. But a measure of comfort had been superimposed. There were odd squares of carpet, a comfortable armchair and a TV set. Inspector Cook's searchers had produced the usual dislocated effect; and a table against one of the walls was stacked with papers, a box file, and a battered portable typewriter. Pollard planted a foot on the rung of a chair and subjected the room to prolonged scrutiny.

'Uncompromisingly single bed, and only one decent chair,' he remarked. 'Rex Lucas written off with finality. Let's go for the stuff on the table. Cook's chaps have been pretty thorough with the cupboards.'

They settled down after lighting the asthmatic but reasonably efficient gas fire. According to their usual custom they worked separately, making an occasional note. Apart from the wheezing and plopping of the fire and an occasional car negotiating Moneypenny Street, the silence was oppressive. Pollard finally broke it.

'Odd,' he said, looking up from an account book. 'Every penny she's spent is booked here, down to a single pinta, but no wages entered up. Somebody stood in for her when she was working for Habgood. Give me the file... Yes, a Mrs Pinfold, 27, Longmeadow Road, described as a respectable widow and a pensioner.'

Toye suggested collusion over an infringement of the earnings rule.

'Not on your life. She never paid on that

113

scale. These accounts of Brown's are damned interesting. She was watching every penny, and putting by in the Post Office. My guess is that she'd had a bit too much hand-to-mouth. Probably left home, came un-stuck in London, and then Lucas walking out put the lid on it. Remember what Habgood said about husband-hunting? And according to Cook, the chaps who took her out dropped her like a hot brick when they realized nothing was on without marriage lines. Pending which, she seems to have been hell-bent on having something in the kitty. I wonder–'

Pollard broke off and was silent for so long that Toye looked round inquiringly.

'Petty blackmail? Mind the shop for free – or else?'

'I think there's just a whiff of it in the air. As a matter of fact it struck me that Mrs Habgood looked a shade relieved when she heard X or Y had been around on Wednesday night. Pure surmise, of course. We've nothing to go on at the moment. A chat with Mrs Pinfold tomorrow may produce something... What have you got there?'

Toye was holding a used sheet of carbon paper up to the light. 'Looks as though Brown may have done typing jobs for people.

There's something here about students and courses.'

'Impound it. It might be a lead.'

They reverted to the papers. Toye began a careful perusal of a notebook recording purchases and sales.

'There's a junk shop near my place where I pick up the odd thing now and again,' he said presently with apparent irrelevance. 'Nice old boy runs it, and we get talking. He says he is feeling the draught like everybody else. Auction prices for job lots are up and customers haven't the cash to pay what'll give you enough profit to live on. If that's general, some of these entries seem a bit out of line.'

Turning over pages, he pointed out recurring small groups of items bought at give-away prices, and resold at a handsome profit. Reference to Inspector Cook's report showed that Annabel Brown attended auctions of the more modest sort and also bought second-hand goods from private individuals. Toye remarked that if she had been putting the screw on people to part with their stuff for next to nothing they wouldn't be keen to come forward.

Pollard agreed rather gloomily and relapsed into silence, staring at a tradesman's calendar in glorious technicolor, portraying Beefeaters at the Tower.

'Let's recap,' he said after an interval. 'The inquest this morning was adjourned for a fortnight, for us to find out why Brown fell down that staircase and killed herself on Wednesday evening. We've been called in because there was a break-in and a theft of books as well, and it seems reasonable to assume that there was a connection. It doesn't follow that X – the chap who broke open the cupboard – deliberately chucked her down. He could have shoved her un-intentionally, in the course of a row. Or she may have slipped quite independently. I know Cook's people couldn't find any reason for an accidental fall, but the reports from the forensic lab aren't in yet. Anyway, the obvious thing for us is to concentrate on finding X.'

Toye agreed. 'What about these chaps she's been going round with in the hopes of hooking one of 'em?' he suggested.

'This is about the only conceivable lead we've got at the moment. Cook's looking into where they all were on Wednesday night. Then there's just the chance of getting something from this Mrs Pinfold tomorrow, I suppose. Then one can't deny that Mrs

Habgood could have been involved: she was virtually on the spot. A motive might possibly come out. But what's nagging at me is that things don't seem to add up where Brown's concerned. Ever since Rex Lucas walked out on her she seems to have been hell-bent on the straight and narrow. Hard work, saving money and husband hunting. Why on earth did she suddenly go for breaking and entering and stealing books?'

'If she was blackmailing people, she was already going crooked,' Toye objected. 'I reckon her savings weren't mounting up fast enough, and she'd learnt enough about fences, earlier on, to be able to flog the books.'

'Could be,' Pollard conceded, still sounding dissatisfied. 'Here, let's knock off for tonight. There doesn't seem to be anything more for us here.'

As he stooped to turn out the gas fire, Annabel Brown's face, seen on his visit to the mortuary, came vividly to his mind. Even death had not quite obliterated its expression of anxiety and tight-lipped determination. A one-track mind, he thought...

Standing with his back to the mantelpiece and his hands in his trouser pockets, he watched Toye carefully filing the notes they had made.

'I've got a nasty feeling that we'll end up with a report of insufficient evidence to determine what led to deceased's fatal fall, etc. etc.,' he said. 'Admission of failure, in other words.'

Toye replied that it wouldn't surprise him, but added with his habitual caution that you never knew what you'd unearth, once you started digging.

Mrs Pinfold had pouched pink cheeks. She wore a bright blue jumper and her skirt was little more than knee length. Without realiing it, Pollard retained the traditional image of an old age pensioner, and was momentarily taken aback. Then he realized that she was frightened and also rather stupid.

'I hope this early call isn't inconvenient,' he said pleasantly. 'We wanted a word with you, and thought you might be going out for the week-end shopping, or to a morning job, perhaps.'

'Oh, I don't go out to work, not as a rule,' she replied with a hint of umbrage. 'I don't need to. Please step inside.'

Pollard and Toye negotiated a three-piece suite which took up most of the small front room's floor space, and waited while Mrs

Pinfold switched on a heater.

'Please to sit down,' she said hastily, and perched uncomfortably forward in one of the armchairs. Pollard took the other, and Toye installed himself in a corner of the settee and took out his notebook.

'Well,' Pollard said in a friendly tone, picking up the thread of the conversation, 'most of us can do with a bit of extra cash these days, can't we? Let me see, you took charge of Mrs Lucas's shop for three afternoons a week, didn't you?'

'That's right,' she said, eyeing him uneasily.

'What did she pay you, Mrs Pinfold?'

The question evoked a desperate resistance. 'I don't see as you've any call to ask me. Earnings is private, so long as you keep under the limit, and that I did.'

'This is it,' Pollard said. 'You see, as the police officers carrying out the inquiry into Mrs Lucas's death, we've been through her papers and account books.' He paused deliberately, and bluffed. 'What was the hold she had over you, Mrs Pinfold, that you agreed to work for her under those conditions?'

To his relief she made no attempt to challenge his knowledge of the terms of her employment, but gaped at him, as if stunned by police omniscience. Then she began to sob, her face puckering. 'Soon as I knew she was dead, I thought... I thought I'd be safe, an' n-now the p'lice knows...'

Bit by bit her sordid and pathetic story came out. The late Mr Pinfold had always seen to everything. After the traumatic experience of his sudden collapse and death in the street just over a year ago, she had at first found coping with life on her own completely unnerving, and developed a whole range of irrational dreads, such as noises in the night, burst pipes and the electric going on fire. Worst of all had been the fear, stimulated by continually rising prices, of not being able to pay her way. She had taken to going round the supermarkets for special offers, trying to save a penny here and a penny there...

'Suppose we help you over the next bit,' Pollard suggested. 'Did you suddenly, one day, without really thinking what you were doing, slip something into your shopping bag instead of the store's basket?'

Mrs Pinfold gave him another stupefied stare at this penetration. 'I'll never know what came over me,' she gulped. 'Tin of chopped ham, it was. The small size.'

Apparently, no one had noticed, but just

after she had gone out into the street there had been a hand on her arm. She had swung round in terror, and found herself looking at Annabel Lucas. Too agitated and inexperienced to threaten a counter-charge or parry questions, she had fallen an easy victim to blackmail. Her unpaid servitude had started immediately, to last for almost a year.

'I made out to the neighbours I was doin' it for the money and for a change from bein' on me own, like. Oh, God, sir, don't take me to court now, along o' what I did. I've been through 'ell.'

'Listen,' Pollard said. 'Shoplifting's an offence, and you know you did wrong. But Mrs Lucas was the only witness of it, and she's dead. You've nothing to worry about now.'

The fresh colour had ebbed from Mrs Pinfold's face. It was tear-stained and blotchy, and her age had abruptly asserted itself in its sagging contours. A woebegone figure, she looked at him incredulously. 'But you knows – and 'im.' She indicated Toye, impassive in his corner.

'We couldn't care less about your slip-up,' Pollard said robustly, 'could we, Inspector? We came to see you to find out what sort of a woman Mrs Lucas was, and you've given us some useful help. That wasn't her real name, by the way. She wasn't married to the man who came down from London with her. She was Annabel Brown.'

The information had an astonishingly tonic effect on Mrs Pinfold's collapsed morale.

'The dirty tart!' she exclaimed, hitting back in satisfied consciousness of her own status of honourable widowhood.

Pollard hastily cashed in with questions about the running of the shop, callers and letters, but learnt nothing new. On the previous Wednesday, Annabel Brown had arrived by car at half-past eight in the morning and had summarily ordered her victim to go back with her and take over for the whole day.

'Any letters by the second post?' Toye asked.

Mrs Pinfold shook her head. No callers, either; not even salesmen trying to get orders for shop fittings and suchlike. Just a few customers. There hadn't seemed to be any end to the day, and it had been cold as Christmas, with that miserable little fire with only one bar...

'So that was the last time you saw Annabel Brown?'

'Last time to speak to, it was.'

There was an electric silence.

'But you saw her again?' Pollard asked, trying to keep urgency out of his voice. 'When was that?'

'When I was cuttin' through Moneypenny Street on me way to the Women's Circle. Wednesday evening it meets, up to the Methodists. Nice and warm in their 'all, and the minister makes you welcome. Shakes your 'and when you goes in...'

'What time was this?' Toye demanded, no longer able to restrain himself.

After a good deal of circumlocution, Mrs Pinfold decided that it was between ten- and quarter-past six. The Women's Circle met at half-past, and first comers got the seats by the radiators. It was just as she turned into Moneypenny Street that she saw Mrs Lucas, as she called herself, come dashing out of the shop, slamming the door shut after her. Then she'd gone running off towards the High Street like a madwoman.

'Mrs Pinfold, why didn't you tell the policeman who came to see you on Thursday about this?' Pollard asked her.

'He never arst, only what time I shut the shop and went 'ome,' she replied, sounding aggrieved. 'Anyways, I were that cold an' tired I never give it a thought, seein' as we 'adn't spoken.'

In order to forestall comment on the interviewing technique of the local force by an outraged Toye, Pollard got hastily to his feet and engineered a speedy departure.

'Feeling better, now you've blown your top?' he inquired, as they got into the Hillman. 'This is our first real break, you know. We'll get Cook to have Mrs Pinfold's statements checked, but I swear she told us the truth on all counts. We know for sure now that Brown was a blackmailer, but what is a damn sight more interesting is that headlong dash out of the shop. How does it tie up with the break-in? Let's have a look at the street plan.'

Toye produced it. It showed that the garage at which Annabel Brown had left her car was roughly five minutes' walk from the shop.

'According to Cook, she turned the car in for its check-up just on six,' Pollard said. 'So she got home at roughly five past. Between ten and quarter past, Mrs Pinfold sees her belting out and heading for the High Street. How long would it have taken her to get to the Athenaeum?'

Toye objected that there was no proof that she had gone straight to the Athenaeum, but if she had, she would have landed up there about twenty-five past six, keeping up a good pace.

'Well, let's assume she did. If she crashed down that staircase while Mrs Habgood was beating up egg whites somewhere about ten to seven, that leaves – say – twenty-five minutes for Brown to go to ground behind the oil tank, crawl about on the floor by the table, and finally go up to the gallery and decide which books to pinch. How's that for timing?'

They agreed that it seemed a feasible programme.

'Right,' Pollard said. 'We'll go on from here. The thousand-dollar question is what sent her tearing out of the shop again so soon after getting home.'

They ruled out a return to the garage to fetch something left in the car. It shut at six, and she could not have expected to find it still open at nearly twenty past.

'Message?' Toye suggested. 'There wasn't a phone at the shop but somebody could have dropped a note in the letterbox after Mrs Pinfold went off at five.'

'A message from *X*?' Pollard said thoughtfully. 'In some agreed code, saying that the break-in was on? If so, why did she hang about behind the oil tank when she got to the Athenaeum? I wonder if she had blackmailed X into doing the job and was checking up on him before going in for some pickings herself?'

Toye thought this an ingenious but complicated idea. Besides, would Brown really have wasted time crawling about looking for an ear-ring, or something, when she got there?

'God only knows what extraordinary things people do,' Pollard replied with feeling. 'Look here, time's getting on. We'd better go round to the library and see how the boys are making out over dabs and whatever.'

Strickland and Boyce had just finished testing the *trompe-l'œil* for fingerprints. They reported that it was plastered with them at the spot where you gave it a push to go through. Most of the dabs were a man's, different from any they'd found so far; but a set of X's, in his rubber gloves, were superimposed. There were none of Annabel Brown's on the library side, but some on the boiler house side, with X's, where they'd pushed the door to go in.

'She didn't need to go out again, of course,' Strickland concluded succinctly.

'What I can't get over is why she didn't wear gloves,' Toye said.

'Thought she'd be able to wipe clean everything she'd touched?' Boyce suggested. 'People haven't a clue that it's next door to impossible.'

There was a sudden shout from Pollard, who had gone through the *trompe-l'œil* into the boiler house.

'What do you make of these?' he asked, as Toye and the two technicians crowded in.

He pointed to two parallel white scrapes on the flagged floor, at an angle of roughly forty-five degrees to the boiler, and quite close to it. They were about sixteen inches long, and eighteen inches apart.

Toye bent to examine them more closely.

'Fresh, from the look of the rest of the floor,' he said.

'Got it!' Pollard exclaimed triumphantly. 'At least, I think so. Measure one of those stacking chairs, will you? Don't touch the metal frame, whatever you do.'

The measurements coincided exactly. The topmost chairs from the two stacks were carefully lifted by Strickland and Boyce, and carried into the library to be tested for fingerprints. Clear impressions came up on the smooth metal, the result of handling

127

them. In addition, the chair from the stack nearer to the boiler house inner door had another set of prints. Strickland straightened up and grinned.

'Same rubber gloves as the chap wore to bust the cupboard open, sir,' he said.

Boyce suppressed a whistle. Pollard straddled a chair, and rested his arms on the back. Toye remarked that you wouldn't have expected the chap to sit down for a warm, seeing the job he'd got on hand.

'I'm not so sure, you know,' Pollard said. 'It's possible that we've been barking up the wrong tree by taking it for granted that he came in from the yard. Suppose he slipped through from the library, some time on Wednesday, and lay up all snug till the place closed? Of course, he had to get out into the yard when he left, but we're assuming for the moment that Brown had fixed that, having had access to the key board in the flat.'

'She was on duty all day Wednesday. On her own, some of the time, you'd think. A place like this wouldn't have all that number of people coming in.'

Pollard, who had a photographic memory, screwed up his eyes.

'Look over on that desk, Boyce,' he said. 'I

noticed a book you sign when you come in to read or look things up. It might be worth finding out who was here on Wednesday. Somebody might have noticed who else turned up.'

Four members of RLSS had signed on the previous Wednesday. Pollard took the book and went in search of Alastair Habgood, whom he found in the office. The librarian looked strained and tired, but on hearing what Pollard had to say he was at once interested.

'Good Lord, that possibility never struck me,' he said. 'Yes, Annabel was on duty all last Wednesday. My wife just relieved her for a short lunch break. May I have a look at the book?'

He took it and ran his eye over the last entries.

'Of course, one doesn't know when these people came in or how long they stayed,' he went on. 'J. B. Alton is in his eighties, and deaf. He comes to track down elusive references in "Ximenes"-type crosswords, and wouldn't notice if the Grand Cham of Tartary walked through the library. F. Richards – now he's a very worthy type from the College of Education, doing a thesis on local industrial archaeology. He'd have been down in the end bay on the right, and you can't see much from there. R. J. Catterick's not very hopeful. He'd have been at the map table with his back to the room, plotting the route for this years Railston.'

'This year's what?'

'Sorry. An RLSS tradition, started by a chap called Railston in '02. A ten-mile hike on Boxing Day, regardless of the weather. You'd be surprised what a crowd turns up.'

'Great heavens!' ejaculated Pollard.

'Quite. It's one of the rare occasions when I'm thankful for my groggy leg. The leader – Catterick, this year – has to make sure that they fetch up at a pub at lunchtime, and get back before dark, of course. No, I think your best bet is Miss Escott. She'd probably have been here most of the day. She's writing a history of RLSS.'

'Escott? Is that the woman Annabel Brown left with on Wednesday evening?'

'Yes. She's a member of the Founder's family – a descendent of his younger son, I believe, and dead keen on RLSS and this place. She's been working in London for a good many years, and came back to Ramsden when she retired recently. It's been her life's ambition, one gathers, and she bought a small house here a few years ago. Nice woman. I'm sure you'll find her helpful and absolutely reliable. Shall I look up her address for you?'

'We've got it in the file, thanks,' Pollard told him. 'We were going to interview her, anyway, as she left here with Annabel Brown on Wednesday night, but this line we're following up on who was in here during the day makes her more of a priority. Before we go, could I just check up with Mrs Habgood about the lunch hour?'

Laura Habgood, called down to the office by the house telephone, came in with her habitual brisk cheerfulness, but Pollard noted the dark shadows under her eyes. She stated, without hesitation, that both Mr Alton and Mr Catterick were in the library when she relieved Annabel but both left soon afterwards. No one else had come in before Annabel returned from lunch.

Pollard thanked her for this information, and after being briefed on the route, left in the Hillman with Toye for Alma Cottages. The day's developments had so far been encouraging. Whatever the outcome of the inquiry, a good deal of ground had to be covered, and he felt that at least some headway was being made. Progress through streets crowded with Saturday morning shoppers was slow and he found the delay irritating. At last Toye extricated the car from the town centre, and turned into Alexandra Road.

Pollard leant forward.

'Those small houses on the left, from the look of them, I should think,' he said, and began to open the passenger door as Toye slowed down.

A couple of moments later he was standing on the pavement, looking in surprise at an estate agent's 'For Sale' notice in the small front garden of Number One, Alma Cottages.

'Funny Mr Habgood didn't know she was selling,' Toye commented, joining him.

They walked round to the front door. A notice on the step, weighted down by a stone, requested 'No milk until further notice'.

'Damn!' Pollard said. 'She's gone away. Let's see if the people next door have got her address.'

The door of Number Two, Alma Cottages, was opened by a fretful woman of indeterminate age, who eyed them suspiciously.

'I'm sure I don't know where Miss Escott's gone off to,' she said ''Tisn't neighbourly, going off without a word like that. Nobody likes an empty house next door, and not knowing when people are coming back. Keeps you on the listen all the time, with all the burglaries we've been having here in Ramsden. If it's the house you're after, the agent's name's on the board.'

'Has it been up for sale long?' Pollard asked.

'The man came yesterday and stuck that board up in the garden. You could've knocked me down with a feather. Never a word about it to her next-door neighbour. That's when I found out she'd gone away, seeing all the windows shut and that notice to the milkman on the step.'

Pollard thanked her and they withdrew, shutting the gate carefully, aware of being watched off the premises from behind the front-window curtains of the little houses. He looked at his watch. 'It's past one,' he said. 'What'll you bet that Henry Moggs Estate Agent, has closed down for the weekend? There's a telephone kiosk along there on the right.'

The only reply to his call was the persistent ringing tone.

'Damn!' he said, returning to the car. 'We'd better consult Cook.'

Chapter 6

Inspector Cook saw no particular significance in Evelyn Escott's absence, or in the fact that her house had been put up for sale.

'Put it this way, Mr Pollard,' he said, planting his hands, palms downwards, on his desk. 'The lady's not young, not by a long chalk, and she was knocked down in the street and her handbag taken, Wednesday night. Then, Thursday morning, I go along and tell her that a friend she was talking to only the night before's been found dead at the Athenaeum under suspicious circumstances. Passed clean out, like I said, Miss Escott did. It seems natural enough to me that she'd feel like a day or two away to get over it all. I reckon she's gone to friends.'

Pollard admitted that this interpretation made sense.

'All the same,' he said, 'after what Mr Habgood told me about her, it seems a bit surprising that she's selling her house. He certainly didn't know anything about it. He said she bought it some years ago for her retirement, and that she'd always wanted to come back to Ramsden, and take an active part in this Society her family founded.'

'There's plenty of other houses in the town,' Inspector Cook pointed out. 'Granted the property market's come off the top, but if she bought some years back she'd make a tidy profit selling now. Maybe she's planning to move to something a bit more run-of-the-mill, with lower rates. There's a preservation order on Alma Cottages, though God knows why. Poky little places and nothing to look at, not as far as I can see.'

'Is Miss Escott the same family as Escott & Co., the estate agents?' Toye asked. 'I've noticed a lot of their boards around.'

'That's right. They're an old Ramsden family. The Super was talking about them last night. She's first cousin to Mr Colin Escott, who's head of the firm now, and pretty warm. It was his old man built it up into a real going concern, and it seems he'd no use in the world for his younger brother, Miss Escott's dad, who could never hold a job down and was always on his beam ends. I doubt if she ever sees her cousins – or wants to. You said Moggs was selling her place, didn't you?'

'Yes.'

'She isn't even selling through the family firm, then … Moggs is in a much smaller way of business. Broad and long, I'd say he caters for clients in the lower price range. Very decent chap, though. Would you like us to get on to him and ask for Miss Escott's address? He'll be bound to have it, in case somebody comes up with an offer.'

Pollard considered. 'Well, yes, we would. According to Mr Habgood, she was working in the Athenaeum library all day last Wednesday, and we're on to a new idea about how X got into the place.'

He went on to describe the marks on the floor of the boiler house and X's gloved fingerprints on the metal frame of the stacking chairs. On this occasion, Inspector Cook was much impressed.

'Well, that's a break-through, if you like,' he said. 'Wish my chaps hadn't missed it. Reckon they saw the marks but didn't use their imagination the way you did, Mr Pollard. Going back to Miss Escott, we'll be glad to get in touch with her ourselves. Her handbag's turned up. A refuse collector found it in a carton put out by one of the shops in the town centre. Cleaned out, of course, but we're interested in the dabs on it. There was another snatch about an hour later that same evening, but the woman managed to hang on to hers. Says it was quite a kid, but he beat it and got away.'

Pollard and Toye were sympathetic on the problems of juvenile delinquency, then finally went off to the room allotted to them, to deal with the backlog of paperwork. It was a bleak little box, with an outlook across the car park to a row of boarded-up houses awaiting demolition. Pollard looked around with distaste. The fortunate Moggs was probably off for the week-end, or on the golf course. At home, Jane would be setting off for Wimbledon Common with the twins, hoping to use up some of their almost inexhaustible supply of energy...

He jerked himself back to the uncongenial present as Boyce and Strickland appeared, and the team settled down to a detailed study of the photographed fingerprints from the library and boiler house. It soon became clear that while these confirmed the statements of the Habgoods and Clare Fenner in all respects, and also the preliminary findings of Inspector Cook's men, they produced no fresh information on the activities of Annabel Brown, X and Y. Annabel had come in through the boiler house, after X and before Y, crawled about on the floor round the librarian's table, gone up the spiral staircase, examined books lying on the gallery floor in front of the cupboard forced by X, and finally returned to the top of the staircase. Just below this, there were clear signs of a frantic but ineffective attempt to grab at the rail.

They pored over the blown-up photographs of the boiler house door handle. Strickland pointed out that X had taken a much firmer grip than either Annabel Brown or Y. X's prints, although beneath the other two impressions, were clearer.

'Interesting,' Pollard commented. 'If X was lying up in the boiler house and had the key to let himself out when he'd got the books he wanted, he'd have turned the handle with the usual amount of grip one uses. Now Brown and Y, coming in from the yard, would instinctively have left the door ajar, wouldn't they? Just pushed it to. To have a quick getaway, I mean. No exit for Brown, but Y would have taken hold of the handle when he went out again. Are Y's dabs clearer than Brown's?'

Further examination established that they were, as well as being more numerous. Finally, Pollard threw down the photographs and told Boyce and Strickland to call it a day and make tracks for London and home.

'And you can thank your lucky stars you aren't us,' he added.

The pair grinned and departed jubilantly, and Pollard and Toye began to tackle the pile of assorted documents on the table.

Various alibis had been confirmed, among them Mrs Pinfold's arrival at the Methodist Hall on Wednesday evening. Evidence was also forthcoming of her servitude at Annabel Brown's shop. The latter's associates in the receiving of stolen goods were also out of the picture. The Yard reported that they had spent the evening in a Camden Town pub, incidentally observed by a plain clothes man who was shadowing a suspected drugs pusher. The Yard also reported that, so far, no information on Annabel Brown's early life had come to light. Local inquiries had satisfactorily accounted for the whereabouts of her former male escorts from Ramsden and its neighbourhood at the time of her death.

The reports from the forensic laboratory were equally unhelpful. There was nothing on the soles and heels of her shoes, or about their state of wear, to account for her having slipped on the staircase, and both supporting straps were still fastened and intact.

Pollard pushed the typed sheet across the table to Toye and began to read the analysis of the dust and fragmentary matter removed by suction from the treads of the staircase.

'"Eye of newt and toe of frog",' he muttered.

Toye looked up with a startled expression.

'Only a quote from Macbeth,' Pollard reassured him. 'Recipe of the witches' hell brew. The analyst chap's nearly as good, though. Just listen to this ... decomposed calfskin ... wing of common house fly ... short, black animal hair ... portion of awn – hell, what's that? – of *Clematis vitalba* (commonly known as Old Man's Beard or Traveller's Joy) ... not much joy for us, that's plain. Here, wade through it yourself.'

Silence descended once more, ultimately broken by Toye. 'Whoever lifted the books seems to be sitting on 'em,' he remarked.

'There's a chit here from the booksy boys at the Yard,' Pollard replied, hunting through a batch of papers. 'Total value about four thousand, they say: hardly worth bothering about, in fact. Cook says there are no outstandingly valuable single items in the library. The best things they've got are complete runs of nineteenth-century natural histories with fine illustrations, and you could hardly carry off twenty or thirty volumes under your arm. Did I tell you that the whole set-up was on the point of folding after the war when the present Chairman – a chap called Westlake – found the original manuscript of a previously unknown sonnet by the poet John Donne? It fetched a cool hundred thousand at auction.'

'And who's John Donne when he's at home?' Toye demanded, in a tone of mingled stupefaction and outrage.

'An unusual type of clergyman who lived in the seventeenth century. I don't think you'd altogether approve – come in!'

A combined knock and opening of the door precipitated a purposeful Inspector Cook into the room.

'The lad who mugged Miss Escott's been brought in,' he announced. 'Caught in Woolworth's, taking a purse out of a woman's shopping basket. We've taken his dabs, and they're on Miss Escott's handbag, but he swears he was in Abbot's Green at seven on Wednesday night, when the second snatch happened. So we thought you'd like to come in on it. His mother's here. Proper bitch.'

'Lead on,' Pollard said, already on his feet. 'All we're doing at the moment is landing up in dead ends.'

Mother and son were sitting as far apart as the area of the interviewing room allowed, as if bent on disowning one another. Pollard experienced a sudden wonder and pity that their original biological unity could have evolved into such alienation in the short space of the boy's life.

Flo Dibble's diminutive figure was huddled into a tweed overcoat several sizes too large for her. Worn slippers suggested a hasty departure from home. The roughened skin of her face was shiny, and she sat with a beaten look, her workworn hands tightly clasped. Ernie, in a navy blue anorak and clumsy, scuffed shoes, sat blinking in the strong light, looking white and pinched, with a runny nose.

'These police officers are Superintendent Pollard and Inspector Toye of Scotland Yard, Mrs Dibble,' Inspector Cook announced. 'They want a word with Ernie about last Wednesday night.'

She stared dumbly at Pollard and made no reply to his polite good evening. He drew up a chair and, sitting down, addressed himself to the boy.

'Ernie,' he said, 'if you've been breaking the law here in Ramsden, it's not my business. Inspector Toye and I aren't one bit interested. We want to see you, though, because we think you can help us in the job we've been sent down from the Yard to do. Got that?'

Ernie sniffed. His mouth fell open slightly.

'Good,' Pollard went on, rightly interpreting this as a sign of surprise and gratification. 'Now, after you'd thrown away the handbag you took from that lady in Alexandra Road last Wednesday evening, what did you do next?'

'Borta ice-cream,' Ernie admitted cautiously.

'With the money 'e stole!' Flo Dibble interrupted shrilly.

'Where did you buy it?' Pollard pursued, ignoring her.

'Shop in South Street.'

'Sercombe's Snack Bar?' asked Inspector Cook.

''Sright.'

'What did you do then?'

'Ate'n, walkin' along.'

'Which way did you go?'

Pollard patiently extracted Ernie's route. It was clear that he was increasingly reluctant to describe it as it reached the neighbourhood of Abbot's Green.

'Come on, old chap,' he said encouragingly. 'This is just where we want you to help us. Did you go into the Green itself?'

''E 'adn't got no call to go inter the Green, where I've worked respectable seven year an' more. 'Tis 'is father's bad blood comin' out in 'im, for all I've toiled and struggled–'

Pollard turned and fixed her with a look which had the effect of making her outburst tail off. She shrank back a little.

'Far better that Ernie's difficulties should come out,' he said quietly. 'We can help him to cope with them now. Don't interrupt me again, Mrs Dibble, please. Now Ernie, let's get this straight, shall we? Do you remember what time it was when you bought your ice-cream?'

Surprisingly, Ernie did. There had been a clock on the wall behind the counter in Sercombe's Snack Bar, saying twenty-five past six.

'Right. Now you're a Ramsden chap and must know the town pretty well. How long do you think it took you to walk from the snack bar to Abbot's Green?'

This question seemed to present difficulties, and Pollard tried another about possible striking clocks.

'I 'eard the parish church strike the 'arf 'our afore I got ter the Green. In Bridge

Street, I was.'

After a brief discussion about distances with Inspector Cook, Pollard came to the conclusion that Ernie must have turned into Abbot's Green at about 6.35 p.m. Possibly a few minutes later.

'Inspector Cook's told you that somebody tried to grab another lady's handbag in West Street on the other side of the town at quarter to seven, Ernie,' he said. 'If you really were in Abbot's Green when you say you were, that somebody couldn't have been you, could he? It's up to you to prove you were in the Green, then, isn't it? Did you meet anybody when you walked round?'

Looking hunted, the boy shook his head and dragged the sleeve of his anorak across his nose.

'Did you see anyone there?'

'I seed a chap walkin' away on t'other side.'

'Would you know him if you met him again?'

'Too far orf, 'e wur.'

Pressed for details, Ernie could only say that the man wasn't tall or short – just ordinary, walking fast and carrying a bag. Asked what sort of bag, he pointed to a briefcase on a chair.

'When you saw this man,' Pollard said, trying to sound almost casual, 'did you notice if he came out of the place where your Mum works? You know it, don't you? The big place, with doors beside it into a yard.'

'Yeah, I knows 'un. No, 'e wur a fair step past 'un,' Ernie replied without hesitation.

'Were the doors into the yard open or shut?'

'Open, both of 'em.'

'I expect you went in yourself, to have a look round, didn't you?'

Ernie stiffened perceptibly. 'I never. Didn't put a foot in the bloody yard.'

The vehemence of the reply brought Pollard sudden illumination. 'No,' he agreed, 'I don't think you did, Ernie. You tried that big brass door knob on the front door, didn't you? It turned, and you slipped inside. That's what happened, isn't it?'

The boy gave a brief nod and looked away.

'I'm orf 'ome,' Flo Dibble shrilled, addressing herself to Inspector Cook. 'Fetchin' the pound odd 'e says 'e took, an' them stamps 'e gave 'is little brother, sayin' 'e 'ad 'em from school. Stolen goods in me 'ouse 'll bring down a curse, more'n what we've got already.'

147

Cook and Pollard exchanged glances.

'Have you any objection to Superintendent Pollard's asking Ernie some more questions while you're away, Mrs Dibble?' the Inspector inquired.

'Ask 'un what yer like. You'll get naught but lies.'

'Right, then. We'll run you home and bring you back.'

The atmosphere eased with Flo's departure. Pollard re-crossed his legs, folded his arms and adopted a more conversational tone.

'When you were inside that place, Ernie,' he said, 'something scared the living daylights out of you, didn't it? We want you to tell us what it was. You'll feel a lot better when you've got it off your chest, you know.'

Ernie whimpered, and once more dragged his sleeve across his face.

'I didn't do nuthin'. I never touched nuthin'.'

'All right, we'll buy that. Did you see something that scared you, then? No? Heard something frightening?'

At last, with infinite patience, he got at the facts. The latch of the door with the funny handle had made an awful noise. There had been moving about inside the room, a sort of scuffling. Somebody screeched and called out. There were some bangs, then a big crash. '…And then a door shut, quiet like.'

'What did you do then?' Pollard asked.

'I wur afeared to run fer it, thinkin' I 'eard a car. Then I wur that scared I 'opped it, an' ran fer the bushes over the road.'

'Was there a car outside?'

'I couldn't see none.'

Pollard paused.

'Ernie, you're being a lot of help,' he said encouragingly. 'Now, this question I'm going to ask you is specially important. Don't answer till you've had time to think carefully. While you were in the bushes, did anybody come out of the door, or the yard, or go into either of them?'

'A girl came along in a car. Drove straight into the yard, an' a woman came runnin' out of the 'ouse and there wur a lot o' kissin' an' 'ugging'?'

'What happened then?'

'She locked 'er car an' took 'er bag an' they went in the 'ouse.'

'Did they shut the doors?'

'Yeah.'

Pollard inquired about the church clock and learned that it had struck seven before the girl drove up. After the two women had disappeared into the house, Ernie had emerged from the bushes and made his way home, getting back just before his mother returned.

Sounds outside announced the return of Flo Dibble. She was ushered into the room by a constable, and slammed a pound note and a small semi-transparent envelope on to the table.

'I'm not sayin' it's all 'e took, mind,' she said.

'Was there anything else, Ernie?' Inspector Cook asked, pushing the envelope towards Pollard and Toye.

'Pen,' the boy replied, glancing at the table.

'What did you do with the pen?'

''E must've fallen outer me pocket when I wur in the bushes. I felt for 'un on the way 'ome, and 'e wur gorn.'

Ignoring Flo Dibble's snort of disbelief, Inspector Cook promptly dispatched a constable to make a search. He cleared his throat. 'Anything more you'd like to ask Ernie, Mr Pollard?'

'No thanks, Inspector. He's helped on our inquiry by being so frank about last Wednesday evening, you know.'

'That'll go on record, Mr Pollard. Before

150

you go, I regret that Mr Moggs won't be available until tomorrow night. He went off in his car and the house is shut up.'

'Oh, thanks very much for finding out. Good evening, Mrs Dibble.'

She made no reply, and the Yard pair went out. As Toye turned from shutting the door of their temporary office, Pollard looked in astonishment at the excitement in his normally solemn face.

'What's bitten you?' he demanded.

'Those stamps…'

'What about 'em?'

'I reckon they're worth thousands. The top one in the packet's a Mauritius twopenny blue. I swear it is!'

'How the devil do you know?' Pollard asked incredulously.

'My eldest's mad keen. He's built up quite a decent little collection. Reads books on 'em and I've glanced at one or two.'

Pollard had a brief vision of the Toye family's estimable private life, incorporating worthwhile hobbies. He stared at Toye.

'If you're right, it's damned rum. Why on earth does the Escott woman carry around stamps worth thousands in her handbag? Not that it need have anything to do with what we're supposed to be investigating. All the same… Hell! Come in!'

He swung round irritably as the door opened, this time to admit Superintendent Daly, with slightly squared shoulders.

'Sorry to butt in, Mr Pollard, but the fact is, Mr Westlake is asking for a word with you. He's Chairman of the Trustees of the Ramsden Literary and Scientific, and of our Bench, too. And the most valuable book that's gone is one of his.'

Pollard groaned.

'OK, Super. Bring him along. I know how it is – only too well!'

Chapter 7

As an obviously relieved Superintendent Daly went out, Pollard turned to Toye.

'So what? Local king-pin? Fancies himself as an amateur sleuth? Wants us to drop everything and go all out to find his blasted book? Any more of this, and he's got another think coming – p.d.q., too!'

'You said this morning we'd be seeing him as soon as we could get round to it,' Toye pointed out reasonably. 'On the chance of picking up something about the party.'

Pollard grimaced at him hideously, as footsteps came along the passage. The next moment, he found himself confronting a tall white-haired man in Harris tweeds, who came forward with hand extended.

'Superintendent Pollard? I'm Westlake. It's good of you to see me. I won't waste your time, I promise you.'

Avoiding Toye's eye, Pollard introduced the newcomer and organized seating. He recognized the type: a shade authoritative from a lifetime of public responsibility and assured social status, but too experienced to be inflated with self-importance. Dead straight in his dealings. Sometimes a bit unimaginative. Pollard sensed, from numberless encounters with witnesses in the past, that here was someone who felt obliged to give the police information, but was reluctant to do so because of an existing loyalty. He decided to give Westlake time to play himself in.

'As a matter of fact, Mr Westlake,' he said, 'we're grateful to you for turning up here and now. We were going to contact you, for some information about the party at the Athenaeum last Tuesday. I take it that, as Chairman, you'd have been there most of the time?'

James Westlake looked surprised.

'Most of the time, yes. I got there early, but left while there were still a few people around. A bigwig who's just joined the Society had to be given dinner. What particular information do you want?'

'Nothing particular. Just an overall picture of the evening. Anything special that you noticed about people there... Yes, do smoke, by all means.'

There was a short hold-up while James Westlake got a pipe going.

'Right,' he said, puffing contentedly. 'You'd better have the general context first. It was a drinks party to celebrate the centenary of the Ramsden Literary and Scientific Society, of which I'm Chairman at the moment. We got under way soon after half-past six. About 130 people turned up, all members and their guests: we're a bit restricted for space, so it wasn't exactly a public function. I made the inevitable speech, and proposed the health of RLSS. After that, things took the normal course for an affair of this kind: people drifting around and chatting. Nothing in the least out of the way happened, to the best of my knowledge.'

'Thanks,' Pollard said, 'that's got the evening in focus, so to speak. You'll have gathered that we think it's possible that there's a connection between the party and what happened at the Athenaeum the following night. As Chairman, you'll have kept a general eye on proceedings, and may possibly have seen something relevant without realizing it. Just take us through the evening as you saw it.'

'Well, let me think… When the speechifying was over, I stood for a bit talking to Professor Thornley, the bigwig I mentioned just now. He's an Oxford Professor of Social

History. Alastair Habgood, our librarian, was there, too. After a bit I felt I ought to round up the Escott family and introduce them to Thornley. They're the descendants of Evelyn Escott who founded and endowed RLSS.'

James Westlake paused and looked across the table with a grin.

'It was damn hard going! Colin Escott and his wife haven't a clue on what RLSS is about, and Thornley is a complete egghead. Mercifully, Peter Escott, Colin's boy who was up at Cambridge, intervened and took Thornley off to see the ceilings in the Habgoods' flat. They're well-known examples of decorative plaster-work, as you've probably gathered by now.'

Pollard, listening with interest, decided that, on the face of it, the partnership of Professor Thornley and Peter Escott seemed unlikely to have lent itself to funny business with keys.

'After that,' James Westlake went on, 'I started circulating, and talking to all and sundry. I was looking out for Miss Evelyn Escott, another member of the family, and capable of talking Thornley's language up to a point. I ran her to earth and fixed with her to come and be introduced when Thornley came back from the flat. Then I went on doing the round. The *trompe-l'œil* is always a draw and I demonstrated it interminably to various groups of people.'

'That clears up one point, I expect,' Pollard put in. 'There's a recurring set of finger-prints on it which are probably yours, and which we'd like to eliminate. Would you mind if we printed you?'

'Good lord, no! Go ahead.'

Toye produced the necessary apparatus and began operations.

'Carry on, Mr Westlake,' Pollard invited. 'You're giving us just the gen we want.'

'There really isn't much more to say, I'm afraid. Just the mixture as before. When I eventually saw that Thornley and young Escott had come down again, I collected Evelyn and took her along. She and Thorn-ley clicked at once. I left them chatting, and they were still at it when I went back to take him off to dinner at the Castle Hotel. That was just before eight. He's an interesting chap if a bit pedantic, and we nearly missed his train. I dropped Habgood off at the Athenaeum on the way back from the station, but didn't go in again myself... Thanks,' he concluded, accepting a rag from Toye, and beginning to clean his fingertips.

'When I started on the job,' Pollard said, after a short pause, 'I thought it looked pretty straightforward – I couldn't have been more wrong. Unexpected ramifications keep sprouting out. One of them is that *X*, as we're calling the chap who broke into the book cupboard, almost certainly got into the boiler house by way of the library during Wednesday. He spent a considerable time there, sitting on one of your stacking chairs, all nice and cosy by the boiler. One of the people we're anxious to contact is this Miss Evelyn Escott, who was working in the library most of last Wednesday. It's possible that she may have noticed who came in.'

As he talked, Pollard saw a small upward jerk of James Westlake's chin. He's come about something to do with this Escott woman, he thought, and waited. No remark was forthcoming, however, so he went on.

'Of course it would be surprising if there were no link between the break-in and Annabel Brown's death, but up to now there is no conclusive evidence that she was in on the job with *X*. But if she wasn't, it raises the question of how *X*, acting on his own bat, got hold of the key to the door of the boiler house. He had to have it in order to get out after nicking the books. One possibility is

158

that he managed to take an impression of the key at an earlier date and get a duplicate cut. Another is that he managed to abstract the key, unlock the door and put the key back during the party, banking on the fact that it was most unlikely that anyone would discover that the door wasn't locked during the next twenty-four hours. We'd like your opinion on this.'

James Westlake smoked in silence for some moments, a worried look on his usually cheerful face.

'In my opinion it's extremely unlikely that anyone could have pulled it off,' he said at last. 'In the first place, it's generally accepted that members don't go through the *trompe-l'œil*. It's an unusually skilled specimen, and one doesn't want all and sundry messing it about. Besides, the last thing one wants is people going into the boiler house – on safety grounds. The stacking chairs are only needed for large gatherings, so there was no need for any individual to go through and fetch one for personal use: they were all out in the library, anyway. What I'm getting at is that anyone going through alone during the party would have been noticeable, if you get me. There's been a lot of local publicity about the details of the break-in, and if anybody had been seen at the *trompe-l'œil*, I'm pretty confident that we should have heard about it. Another thing is that I myself was standing near it for a considerable part of the evening, either showing people how it worked, or just chatting. Then, of course, getting the key, coming down, and going up to the flat again to replace it, would mean two trips each way: a bit conspicuous for a chap on his own, perhaps. I think it might well have been noticed casually and remembered since.'

'None of this is conclusive,' Pollard said, 'but on the whole I'm inclined to agree with you.'

Silence descended, which he allowed to become prolonged before he broke it.

'Mr Westlake,' he said at last. 'What did you really come to see us about?'

James Westlake removed the pipe from his mouth and contemplated it.

'Evelyn Escott,' he replied. 'Do I take it that you know she's gone away, leaving no address, and having put her house up for sale?'

Pollard nodded.

'Yes,' he said. 'We want to see her, as I told you: we went round there this morning, too late to get the estate agent's office before it closed for the week-end. Inspector Cook tried to contact him for us, but he seems to have gone off into the blue until tomorrow night.'

'Did Cook tell you anything about her past history?'

'A bit, yes. I gather her father couldn't make the grade, and she's had a hard life, more or less disowned by her prosperous relations here.'

'There's more to it than that. She's a natural academic, if you follow me. All her inclinations are that way. The tragedy was that she didn't get to a university, but was given a third-rate secretarial training and pushed out to earn at the earliest possible moment. Eventually her parents died, and by sheer determination she got herself to London, went to evening classes, and on pure merit managed to get and hold down good jobs. But all through, her one aim was to get back here with enough to live on and identify herself with RLSS, founded by her forebear, old Evelyn Escott. We welcomed her, of course, and encouraged her to write a little history of the Society. She was thrilled to bits.

'As I told you, I put her on to Thornley. He's a decent old scout, and took to her. Gave her useful advice, and a general bibliography, and told her to keep in touch, and send her stuff along for him to vet. I got all this from him over dinner on Tuesday night. She spent the whole of Wednesday working in the library. It wasn't until Friday that I managed to ring her and ask her how she was, having heard that she'd been knocked down and had had her bag snatched on Wednesday night. I rang twice and got no answer, and again on Saturday morning. Then I felt a bit uneasy, went along to the house and saw that it was up for sale. I was staggered, then realized that all the windows were shut; also I found a note stopping milk deliveries.

'By this time I began to feel really disturbed, and decided to go and see Moggs, the agent. I made a few judicious inquiries, and learnt that Miss Escott had put the property on Mogg's books, telling him she was going away for a few days, and would ring him when she got back. She hadn't given him an address.'

James Westlake paused, as if uncertain about how to go on.

Pollard realized that the moment of truth was imminent. 'And did you leave it at that?' he asked.

'No. I told Moggs – with perfect truth –

that I'm casting around for a small house in these parts for an elderly relative, and thought that Miss Escott's might be suitable. I know him quite well, and as he was just going off in his car for the week-end he offered to let me have the keys, provided I'd undertake to drop them in first thing on Monday.'

'So I gather you went over the house and found no sign of Miss Escott? That must have been a relief. Was there any clue to where she's gone?'

'None, but I had only a pretty superficial look round. However, I did find something which I feel you ought to know about. Perhaps I'd better explain here that I was present in a completely unofficial capacity at the discussion between our CC and Daly and Cook, when the decision was taken to call in the Yard. So I know about the time within which that unfortunate girl could have died, also the fingerprints on the boiler house door handle made by her, X and Y. To come to the point, I found a pair of damp knitted gloves, hung up to dry. Add this to Miss Escott's actions over the past three days, and it suggests to me that she could be Y.'

Pollard clasped his hands behind his head

and sat deep in thought for a few moments. 'The time limit for *Y's* trip to the Athenaeum is roughly from midnight, when the heavy rain set in, and 8.15 a.m., when the body was discovered. Can you think of any conceivable reason for Miss Escott to go round there during this period?' he asked.

'Absolutely none,' James Westlake replied categorically. 'The whole business seems baffling.'

'Another thing, sir,' Toye put in. 'If Miss Escott is *Y,* she couldn't have reckoned on being able to get into the boiler house and the library. It was chance that the wind blew the yard doors open, to start with. Doesn't it look as though she must have gone round to see the Habgoods? You'd think she'd have rung them, if it was all that urgent or, any-way, knocked them up when she got there.'

'I'm not absolutely sure about ringing them,' Pollard said thoughtfully. 'There are quite a lot of older people who don't care about dealing with anything private or very important over the phone. Assuming that Miss Escott is *Y,* my guess is that the idea was to knock up the Habgoods but that something diverted her into the yard, just as it's possible that Brown was diverted if she wasn't in the break-in.'

James Westlake shifted his position abruptly. 'Are you going to ask for a search warrant?' he asked. 'I realize that I've sailed a bit close to the wind.'

'This sort of navigation's bound to be tricky,' Pollard remarked. 'There's always that handy chap, *Information Received*, isn't there? Yes, I think we'd better go along. The gloves are potential evidence and there's no guarantee that Miss Escott won't turn up at any moment.'

Their eyes met. Pollard raised a quizzical eyebrow. James Westlake responded with a rueful grin.

'Right,' he said, getting to his feet.

Strip lighting overhead flooded Evelyn Escott's small kitchen, illuminating the various objects on the table.

'It's a dead cert, sir,' Detective-Constable Neale told Pollard. 'You've only got to look at this glove under the mike. See where a thread's been pulled in the first finger where it's caught on something rough?... Now take a look at the blow-up of the dabs on the door handle your chap did... Bit mucky, with the three lots, but the pattern and that pulled thread stand out like a sore thumb, don't they?'

Pollard and Toye looked, as requested, and agreed. After some further discussion Constable Neale reluctantly departed.

'Where do you propose going from here?' James Westlake asked Pollard, leaning against the sink with hands thrust into his trouser pockets.

'We'd better have a quick look round, I think, in case there's some clue to where Miss Escott's gone. Do you mind waiting?'

'Not in the least. I'll stay in here and keep out of the way.'

A glance into the refrigerator disclosed eggs and fats but no milk or cooked food. Remarking that this suggested a return before very long, Pollard led the way into the tiny hall and stood looking round. The house was scrupulously clean and tidy but upstairs, in Evelyn Escott's bedroom, there were signs of a hurried departure. Drawers were not quite shut and garments had been bundled into a hanging cupboard.

Leaving Toye to investigate further, Pollard went down to the sitting room. Utilitarian, like the rest of the house, he thought, groping for the right adjective. Everything rather depressingly sensible and hardwearing. Colours that didn't show the dirt. He had a quick vision of Jane removing small

166

fingermarks form the white paint, which contributed so much light and brightness to their very ordinary suburban house. Here there wasn't the vestige of a frill. The few pictures were standard reproductions, too well known, and inevitably including Van Gogh's *Sunflowers*. It was difficult to feel that Evelyn Escott found them inspiring. A modest TV set was the nearest approach to an outlay for enjoyment. The whole set-up was the home of someone accustomed, over the years, to count every penny.

He turned his attention to the books. The English classics were in evidence, and there were standard reference books and well-known semi-popular works on aspects of social history. A run of thin, paper-covered books attracted his attention and he pulled out a few. They were intermittent publications by members of the Ramsden Literary and Scientific Society, on subjects relating to the town and the surrounding countryside of Glintshire. *Vestigial Frescoes in the Church of St James the Less, Marlingford,* he read. *The Eglington Earthwork, Pillow Lavas in the Parish of Great Bidding, the Last Polecats of Glintshire...*

Wrenching himself away from this fascinating investigation, Pollard replaced the booklets while reflecting that more and more about less and less had its attractions. In micro-activity of this sort you must surely be able to feel that you really had covered the ground.

The solid writing table in the window had two drawers. In one he found an indexed file of household documents, stationery and some personal letters from acquaintances in London, of no great degree of intimacy. Pollard noted down the writers' addresses and looked through a sparsely filled address book. The right hand drawer was locked. He took a bunch of keys from a pocket and found one which opened the drawer. Evelyn Escott's bank statements showed a steady credit balance of just over £200 since the payment of what must have been the expenses of her move to Ramsden six months earlier. There were neatly docketed personal papers, ranging from Evelyn's birth certificate to a copy of a short, simple will, in which she left everything to the Ramsden Literary and Scientific Society 'founded by my great-great-uncle, the late Evelyn Escott'.

It struck Pollard that there was something rather formidable as well as pathetic about her single-mindedness. He replaced the contents of the drawer, and was relocking it when Toye came in.

'Not a thing for us upstairs,' he said. 'Not one to spend where she needn't, is she?'

Pollard agreed. 'Nothing down here, either, apart from a few addresses in London, which we can put the Yard on to. I shouldn't think she's likely to be at any of 'em. Does she seem to have taken much with her?'

Toye was of the opinion that little more than basic requirements and a change of clothes were missing.

Pollard got up. 'We may as well pack it in, I think,' he said, adding, *sotto voce,* 'we can't talk here.'

In the tiny hall space he glanced at the telephone, remarking that it seemed rather surprising that Miss Escott had gone to the expense of putting one in.

'Sorry to have kept you hanging about, Mr Westlake,' he said, going into the kitchen. 'There's really nothing to show for it, either. Miss Escott seems to have gone away in a bit of a hurry, not taking much with her, which looks as though she'll be back soon. Just one thing you might know: is she a stamp collector?'

James Westlake looked both surprised and

interested. 'Not that I know of. She hasn't shown up at any meetings of the RLSS Philately Section, anyway. I go along to those, being a collector in a small way, myself.'

Pollard subsided on to a chair. 'Has the Society got a collection of its own?' he asked, as casually as he could.

'No, but we've got books on philately for local enthusiasts.'

Damn, Pollard thought. Another dud lead...

'You know,' he said, 'it's impossible not to feel that this odd visit of Miss Escott's to the Athenaeum must be connected with the Society in some way. You're the Chairman. You can't, I suppose, put forward any suggestions? No impending crisis, for instance, that she might have been worrying about?'

James Westlake shook his head. 'I've been sitting here racking my brains about why she went round. To the best of my knowledge and belief there's absolutely nothing out of the ordinary in our affairs at the moment. I–' He broke off as Toye appeared at the kitchen door, holding the telephone directory.

'Excuse me, sir,' Toye said, addressing Pollard. 'I noticed a marker sticking out of this and had a look. It was in at "Hotels" in the yellow pages, and there's one with a tick beside it.'

'"Bella Vista Private Hotel, Beach Road, Southcliffe",' Pollard read aloud. 'Sounds quite modest. Southcliffe's about twenty miles from here, isn't it? It's worth a long shot, I think. Ask for – say – a Mrs Westcott, Toye, and pull out again by apologizing for having rung the wrong hotel.'

As they waited for the call to go through, it struck him that James Westlake was looking preoccupied. It was very quiet, and within seconds of Toye's dialling they could hear the ringing tone at the other end of the line.

'Mrs Westcott,' Toye enunciated clearly. 'W-E-S-T-C-O-T-T, Mrs... No, that's not the name, I'm afraid. I've rung the wrong hotel... So sorry to have troubled you...'

He put down the receiver and joined them. 'They say a Miss Escott is staying in the hotel,' he reported, with characteristic caution but an air of satisfaction.

The others were congratulatory.

'Inspector Cook asked me to get on to him if we ran Miss Escott to earth,' Pollard said. 'Her handbag's been brought in. Naturally, we've got to see her ourselves. I think we'd better suggest that he ring the hotel and say he's sending a car tomorrow morning to bring her up here to identify her property. When she's done that, we say we want a word with her.'

James Westlake frowned slightly. 'She's having a pretty harrowing time, one way and another. Would there be anything against my standing by in case she wants any advice or help?'

'None at all,' Pollard replied. 'I think it's a very sound idea.'

After some further discussion, all three men left the house, James Westlake to drive to his home, and Pollard and Toye to the police station.

'You didn't let on about those stamps in her bag,' Toye said, as they waited at traffic lights.

'No. I've got a hunch, you know, that there's somehow a link with this blasted Society and the Athenaeum, and if I'm right, Westlake's got a sort of vested interest as Chairman of the set-up. It seemed better to keep mum for the moment.'

Much to Pollard's relief, both Superintendent Daly and Inspector Cook were off duty. Acting-Inspector Harris, who was in charge, showed signs of being overawed by having to deal with the Yard, and no questions arose about how Evelyn Escott had been located. He rang her at the Bella Vista Hotel, and reported that she seemed properly thrilled when he told her about the bag and its contents, and would be glad to come up and claim them the next morning.

Pollard thanked him and returned to Toye, who was characteristically reducing the papers on the table in their room to a degree of order. The two men settled down to write up their notes for the case file.

'Thank the Lord that's done!' Pollard said, half an hour later. 'Some day! I simply must knock off for a bit... You look as though a great thought's hit you.'

'I wouldn't be surprised if Mr Westlake doesn't end up by getting sweet on Miss Escott,' Toye remarked decorously.

Pollard stared at him incredulously.

'How do you know he isn't married?' he demanded.

'I chanced to pick up one of those glossy County magazines over in the library,' Toye told him. 'There was a full page photo of him, under "Personality of the Month", and a paragraph about all his public service underneath. It said he was a widower.'

'Becoming the Yard's number one romance expert, aren't you? I refuse to join you in idle speculations, unworthy of a police officer. Here, buzz off and eat, and go to the movies to clear your head. I'm going to ring Jane first, then get a spot of exercise and fresh air when I've had some grub.'

The interlocking complexities of the inquiry into Annabel Brown's death vanished at a stroke as Jane's voice came over the line.

'Plenty of minor roads leading nowhere in particular,' he told her, using their private motoring code.

'Don't tell me you aren't enjoying the driving,' she said. 'It sticks out a mile from your tone of voice. It's art for art's sake, of course.'

'Shut up! We all have our better moments.'

'Well, this definitely isn't one of mine. The twins started chickenpox this morning... No, not really ill... Rose is a bit low this evening. Andrew has exactly six spots, and has scratched the lot... No, not on his face, fortunately... Yes, an awful bore, but it's something to get it over before they start real school, and they've at least synchronized...' The conversation became purely domestic.

When they finally rang off Pollard made for the hotel grill room. He emerged, some time later, feeling considerably restored and had his coffee brought to a quiet corner of the lounge. He drank several cups, but found that it was not contributing much to clarity of thought about the latest developments in the inquiry.

Topics such as the mortgage on the Wimbledon house, and the pay differential between mere Superintendents and Chief Superintendents drifted through his mind like a procession of fair weather cumulus clouds. Then the recent conversation with Jane led him to consider once again his attitude to his professional reputation. Was he really becoming obsessed by his public image, the product of a string of successes in cases blown up by the news media? Jane was almost uncomfortably perceptive... Anyway, he thought, I can still get hooked on a job like this one, without a hope of a headline-hitting solution...

At last he took up the file of the case and began to digest the considerable body of information, acquired to date. Progress was slow, owing to the overwhelming desire for sleep that now descended upon him. Eventually he abandoned the attempt, fetched a coat and went out.

The fog had lifted. It was a cold, frosty night, with stars overhead and a light wind. Almost without thinking, he threaded his

175

way through the streets to Abbot's Green. Here he stood for a time looking at the Athenaeum, and remembering what Alastair Habgood had told him about its history. A sort of repository of centuries of human activity and experience, he thought. The mediaeval gatehouse and the eighteenth-century mansion. Old Escott's vision and inflexible purpose and pig-headedness. The accumulated wealth of men's knowledge and creative achievement on the shelves. The years of decline and dust and the fantastic discovery of the Donne manuscript. And now, violence and death and a frightened boy. History repeating itself, probably, from the time when the gatehouse was func-tional...

The sound of a car turning into the Green broke into these reflections. Acting on a unexplained hunch Pollard stepped back and stood behind some shrubs in the central area. Confirming his hunch the car, a sports model, drew up outside the Athenaeum. The two people inside sat talking for a minute or so, then a young man got out and went round to open the passenger door. Clare Fenner emerged.

Pollard felt glad she had had an evening out, away from the inevitably tense atmosphere of the Habgoods' flat. He watched a restrained farewell and decided that the acquaintance was at an exploratory stage. The young man was not invited in; and after the door had closed behind Clare, he returned to the car and drove off.

The curtained windows of the Habgoods' flat glowed cosily. Pollard realized that he was getting cold, and turned away, making for the hotel. On arrival he capitulated to weariness and, after a quick drink in the bar, went up to bed. He was asleep within minutes of switching off his beside lamp.

He awoke in a state of stress, struggling out of a dream in which he hunted desperately in a darkened building for an unknown object. At last he knew that he was on the brink of finding it, but in the moment of discovery was suddenly engulfed by disaster...

He raised himself, blinked and looked at his watch. It was a quarter to six, and he felt rested and remarkably clear-headed. Fortunately a chronic staff shortage had led the hotel management to provide tea-making facilities in bedrooms. He got up, brewed himself a pot and returned purposefully to bed with the file of the case.

Chapter 8

Two hours later Pollard descended to the hotel dining room, where he found Toye already at breakfast.

'Damn all,' he replied to an inquiry about ground covered on the previous evening. 'My brain simply cut out, so I went for a stroll and then to bed. I slept like the dead until nearly six, since when I've been chewing over the file.'

Toye registered interest.

'I can't expound at the knife and fork stage,' Pollard complained, spearing a sizeable length of sausage. 'We can sit for hours over coffee, from the look of things.'

It was Sunday morning and the dining room, laid up for comprehensive breakfasts, was empty apart from themselves. A waitress who brought a fresh supply of toast looked at them with mingled resentment and curiosity. She hovered briefly, then disappeared through the service door, which closed automatically behind her with a small thud. Finally Pollard pushed his plate aside and poured himself a second cup of coffee.

'If I had to come up with a printable adjective for this job we're on,' he said, taking a piece of toast, 'I'd call it overclued. It's positively lousy with clues. To begin with, there's the unusually complicated setting of Annabel Brown's death: a combined semi-public library, which is the HQ of an active local society, and the home of the librarian and his wife. Twenty-four hours or so before she died, about 130 people were milling all over it. Then there are people involved with the set-up, in various ways which may or may not tie up with the inquiry, like the Habgoods' niece and the wretched Ernie Dibble's mother and Professor Thornley. So, while I was sitting up in bed and swilling cups of tea just now, I tried to ignore all this detail for the moment and concentrate on the basic question: what are we here for? Sounds a bit like the title of a series of sermons, doesn't it?'

Toye, a pillar of his parish church, looked slightly askance, and Pollard hurried on.

'Well,' he said, spooning marmalade on to his plate, 'in case it's escaped your notice, we're here to find out what made Annabel Brown fall down the spiral staircase in the library at the Athenaeum and kill herself. The pathologist and the forensic chaps are *Don't Knows*. No marks of violence on the body, or evidence of heart failure or whatever. No grease or slippery mud on her shoes or the stairs; no structural defects in the staircase. Nothing whatever on the treads to cause a slip. The obvious explanation is that she was started by Ernie's dropping the latch, dashed for the top of the staircase and somehow stumbled. Why don't we send in a report to that effect, Watson?'

'To start with, she'd no call to be there at all,' Toye replied promptly. 'She came in by a door she couldn't have expected to be open, unless she'd done it herself. And there's the funny business of her hiding behind the oil tank, and crawling around on the floor. Then there's *X*, who went in ahead of her, bust open the cupboard and made off with valuable books.'

'And, of course, she'd helped herself to some, too,' Pollard took up. 'The ones Cook's chaps found on the floor with her dabs on 'em. There's also the mysterious visit of *Y*, some time after midnight. *Y* appears to be a respectable maiden lady with a fixation on this Society, who carries very valuable stamps about in a handbag and gets herself mugged.'

'The mugger being this lad Ernie, who makes an unlawful entry into the building, and gives out that he made a clatter and heard scuffling inside the library, somebody calling out, then a crash.'

'Don't forget,' Pollard said, 'that he says he also heard a door shut, quiet like, and was afraid to beat it at once because he thought he heard a car outside. When he did cut and run, he didn't see any car. Nor did he see anybody come out of the building or the yard, though he hung around in the bushes until Clare Fenner arrived at five minutes past seven.'

Toye considered these points. 'I don't see that Ernie's not having seen anybody come out means much,' he said. 'If X pushed Brown down the staircase he could have waited in the boiler house until he thought the coast was clear. It could've been then that he sat by the boiler and the chair made those marks on the floor. And if the boy really heard a door closing, it could have been the camouflaged one, when X went through to the boiler house.'

'Or the door into the flat,' Pollard remarked grimly. 'How do you think Ernie would make out in the box?'

'I don't think he'd be all that easy to

shake,' Toye replied, after further consideration.

'Nor do I. Where the prosecution would press him though, would be how long it was after the door shut that he first thought he heard a car.'

'Mrs H. beating up eggs?'

'This is it.'

They relapsed into silence.

'If anything in the way of a motive turned up, it seems to me the lady would be in a spot,' Toye said presently. 'Do you think Mr Habgood could be in on Brown's death?'

'No.' Pollard was decisive. 'For one thing, there doesn't seem any doubt that he'd been ill all day. Then there's his permanent disability: he'd never have gone to tackle a burglar. And if he arrived in the gallery to see his wife send Brown flying, he'd have had the wits to assume it was an accident and ring for the police ... well, to come to the outcome of my attempts to think straight, it seems to me that there are two immediate priorities. One is to clear up this Escott-Y business and see if there's anything for us in it. The other is to find X. Here, we'd better get cracking.'

The dining room was filling up. Pollard realized that their table was attracting interest, and that the Sunday papers were much in evidence. 'I hope to God we haven't overlooked anything vital,' he said, aware of sudden tension in himself. 'I've got a beastly, nagging feeling that we have.'

Toye followed him soberly out of the room. Past experience had taught him to respect Pollard's hunches.

They had sat for a long time over breakfast, and arrived at the police station only a few minutes before the car bringing Evelyn Escott from Southcliffe. As she was escorted to Inspector Cook's room, Pollard, who was talking to Acting-Inspector Harris, looked at her with interest. His immediate reaction was that her face seemed familiar. Rather a large face, with a good brow and square chin, but unmarred by the bulldozer expression of some women of her age and physical type. Just now it bore signs of both severe stress and unmistakable jubilation.

He watched the short, sturdy figure disappear, then turned to Inspector Harris.

'That's Miss Evelyn Escott,' he remarked, and decided on a long shot. 'Not much like her Ramsden cousins, is she?'

Comment was easily forthcoming. The Colin Escotts were the prosperous branch of the family: Escott & Co., the estate agents. They'd made a proper packet out of the property boom since the war, on top of what they'd got already. Bought a lovely old place a couple of miles out, and done it up regardless.

'There's a son, isn't there?' Pollard asked, stemming a flood of information about one of Colin Escott's more spectacular property deals of recent years.

He learned that young Peter Escott was in the family firm, and none too pleased about it, from all accounts. He'd been away at a posh school, then at Cambridge, where he'd ended up with a poor degree and come away without an idea in his head about taking up a worthwhile career. It seemed his father had had enough of it, stopped his allowance and told him that he could come into the firm and work his way up – or else. Mr Colin Escott might do himself well, but he was a worker, all right. Built up Escott's into a lot more than just a Ramsden firm he had, over the years. Why, Escott's handled property all over the country: real big deals, too, and you even came upon their adverts in the national newspapers.

Pollard returned slowly to his room, once more thinking about Peter Escott. He had certainly been up to the flat on the night of the party and would probably have some idea of the lie of the land – seeing how the family was involved with the place. Was it possible that he was X – at any rate, as far as the book theft was concerned? Valuable books, always provided they weren't too valuable, could be converted into ready cash without excessive difficulty. But there remained the problem of how and when the boiler house key was used...

Still meditating, Pollard arrived and began to put his speculations to Toye. He was still doing so when a knock on the door announced Inspector Cook, with Evelyn Escott in tow.

The jubilation had almost faded from her face; she was looking white and, in a controlled manner, frightened. Almost as if she were preparing to face a firing squad with dignity, Pollard thought. As well as a handbag over her arm, she was gripping a second one tightly. He eased her into a chair drawn up by Toye, and began by congratulating her on the safe return of her property.

'I hear that even your pen has been found,' he said.

'Yes, it has,' she replied briefly.

'Well now,' he said. 'I expect you're tired of being asked about leaving the Athenaeum with Annabel Brown last Wednesday night, but I hope you won't mind just going over the ground once more for our benefit. By the way, were you taken aback to hear that her name was Brown, not Lucas?'

Evelyn Escott looked surprised at this turn in the conversation.

'I – I don't really know. A good many young people are casual about marriage these days.'

'What was your personal opinion of her?'

He sensed a reluctance to commit herself.

'I had very little to do with her. When I am working in the library and need help, I naturally go to Mr Habgood. She wasn't a librarian: only his secretarial assistant on certain days of the week.'

'All the same,' Pollard persisted, 'you must have formed an opinion of her over the past months.'

'I didn't find her congenial. Her attitude to the older members of the Society like myself left a good deal to be desired.'

There was a pause. Evelyn Escott sat as though carved in stone. Acting on impulse, Pollard plunged. 'Don't look like that, Miss Escott. We know you didn't kill her.'

She started, as if from an electric shock. Without looking at Toye, Pollard knew that he had startled him, too.

'You couldn't have, you know,' he continued conversationally. 'The post-mortem established that she was dead before eight o'clock on Wednesday night, and after the police left you at about twenty past six, they parked in the road outside until after seven. If you had come out of your house they would have seen you. By quarter past, the yard doors at the Athenaeum were shut and you couldn't have got in. But we do know that you went round there, either at some time during the night or early on Thursday morning, after the gale had blown the doors open again. Why did you go?'

Evelyn Escott began to shiver uncontrollably. She made no attempt to deny her visit.

'Her cheek was cold,' she said, almost inaudibly. 'I touched it.'

'You could do with a cup of hot coffee,' Pollard said prosaically. 'Toye, see what you can do in the canteen, will you?'

When they were alone, she sat for a few moments, still clasping the second handbag, then suddenly looked up.

'You seem a kind man,' she said, sounding surprised. 'I've never had anything to do with the police before … until I was knocked down, that is … I just don't know what to do.

I'm in a dreadful position.'

'You could tell me about it, if you like. Two heads can be better than one.'

'It's such a long muddly story ... I'm sure you'll think a lot of it very silly...'

Using his powers of persuasion, Pollard managed to get her to talk. His opinion of Evelyn rose as he listened. She touched only briefly, and without self-pity, on her early frustrations. All her working life, she told him, she had wanted to retire to Ramsden and be reinstated as an Escott, in Old Evelyn's tradition. The welcome and encouragement she had found at the Athenaeum had far outweighed the cold-shouldering by the Colin Escotts.

'You see, they're ashamed of me and think me a bore,' she said frankly. 'I just don't fit into their world. My clothes are wrong, and I've had next to no social life of their sort.'

'I shouldn't lose any sleep over that,' Pollard replied. 'You're making a thoroughly worthwhile life of your own here.'

'Up to last Wednesday, I thought I was. Now I seem to have messed everything up. I'd better tell you what happened, I suppose...'

Pollard listened with mounting astonishment to the story of the interference with her papers; Annabel Brown's search of the volumes of the *Extinct Mammalia;* and, finally, Evelyn's extraction of the packet of stamps from the girl's handbag. Toye, returning quietly with cups of coffee, placed one beside her and resumed his seat.

'I still feel I did the right thing,' Evelyn Escott said, rather unhappily, but with what Pollard recognized as unshakeable conviction. 'She had appropriated something which was the Society's property, and I'm a member. Perhaps I ought to have challenged her, there and then. But I just had to do something. If only Mr Habgood hadn't been ill I should have taken the packet straight to him, of course; but as it was, it seemed the most sensible thing at the time to take it home for the night and find out whether it was anything valuable or not. Then I was knocked down, and my bag stolen, as you know.'

'I'm not an authority on stamps,' Pollard said, 'but I know enough about them to be able to tell you that some, at least, of those in the packet are very valuable, and RLSS is going to be very grateful to you.' He watched a look of astonished delight come into her eyes.

'Tell me now,' he went on, 'did you go

round to the Athenaeum very early the next morning to tell Mr Habgood what had happened?'

'Yes, I did. I got there at about a quarter past seven. Of course, I realize now that I ought to have told the police, who came when I dialled 999 on Wednesday night, all about the stamp business. But I just funked it, I'm afraid. You see, I wasn't sure... It seemed so awful to make everything public when it mightn't be necessary after all. I felt I'd come out of it so badly and it would be the end of everything I'd lived for where RLSS was concerned... Moral cowardice... I'm so ashamed, looking back on it ... I pretended to myself that the bag would be found, and whoever took it would only be bothered about the money in it...' Her voice trailed off, with an ominous hint of tears.

'It's important to remember that one's got a body as well as a mind,' Pollard said, 'and they interact. You'd just had a nasty, painful physical attack and were hardly in a state to make difficult decisions. Don't be so hard on yourself, Miss Escott... When did you decide to go round to the Athenaeum?'

'During the night: I didn't sleep much. But I came to my senses and realized that whatever happened to me, personally, I *must* tell the authorities about the whole business. And Mr Habgood seemed the obvious person: he's responsible for the library, you see.'

'You went very early,' Pollard commented, by way of encouraging her to go on.

'Yes. I knew that the cleaner arrived at half-past seven, so the front door would be open; and I thought that I could slip in and up to the flat. But I was too early, and as I could see that the gale had blown open the doors into the yard, I thought I'd stand just inside to get some shelter.'

'What made you go down to the boiler house?'

'The door was banging in the wind. It's always kept locked, and it seemed so extraordinary that I went to see what could have happened.'

'And you went in?' Pollard prompted.

'Yes ... I went in. The boiler seemed all right, so I – I went on into the library. I had a torch, and shone it round. Everything looked quite normal at first; then ... I saw Annabel ... I could see she'd fallen down the spiral staircase, and thought she might still be alive. So ... so I just touched her cheek...'

'Quite right of you,' Pollard said in a

matter-of-fact tone. 'And you found it was stone cold, of course?'

'Yes. Then I behaved disgracefully … panicked … and ran away. I planned to leave Ramsden altogether… Shall I get into trouble for not reporting it to the police?'

'The fact that you didn't will be included in my report, of course, but I don't think you need worry about it too much, Miss Escott. We're grateful to you for being so frank. Now, could you switch your mind over to something quite different? Think yourself back into the party at the Athenaeum last Tuesday, if you can manage it. Did you notice anyone going through the *trompe-l'œil* into the boiler house?'

'Oh, yes. Several people. Mr Westlake – he's Chairman of RLSS – was showing a lot of people how it worked. But I didn't know any of them.'

'And did you, by any chance, go up to the flat during the evening?' Pollard asked.

'Yes, I did. I took a Mr and Mrs Langley to see the ceilings.'

'Were there any other people there?'

Evelyn Escott wrinkled her brow momentarily… 'Yes. Professor Thornley was sketching one of the ceiling motifs in the sitting room. About half a dozen other–'

'Just a moment,' Pollard cut in. 'Was Professor Thornley alone?'

'My cousin, Peter Escott, was just going into the room. Mr Westlake had told me that he – Peter – had taken the Professor up to the flat. I didn't know the other people, but three or four of them joined on when I was explaining about the plaster-work to the Langleys. My party all went back to the library together, as far as I can remember. I don't think anyone was in the flat when we came away.'

Pollard was silent for a few moments.

'Now that the stamps are safely back, Miss Escott, what are you going to do about them?' he asked her.

'I suppose,' she said slowly, 'I'd better face it at once and go round to see Mr Habgood.'

Toye fidgeted unnecessarily with some papers.

'Wouldn't it be better to hand them over to Mr Westlake? He is, after all, the Chairman,' Pollard suggested.

Evelyn Escott looked started. 'Perhaps I ought to, then.'

'Excuse me, sir,' Toye intervened. 'I chanced to notice Mr Westlake just now when I went for the coffee. He may still be on the premises.'

'Quite a coincidence,' Pollard remarked, completely deadpan. 'I wonder if you'd like me to put him very briefly into the picture, Miss Escott? Inspector Toye could be typing out a statement for you to read over, then sign, if you agree it's accurate.'

'I'd be very grateful,' she said, with feeling.

James Westlake was sitting in his car. He leaned over and opened the passenger door.

'This,' Pollard said, 'is a highly condensed version of an almost incredible story...'

When he came to an end, James Westlake remained completely silent for several moments. He finally reacted personally, rather than as Chairman of the Ramsden Literary and Scientific Society.

'She's been through sheer hell, you know.'

'Well, over to you,' Pollard replied. 'These stamps and whatever. By the way, I'm certain one of them is a Mauritius twopenny blue. In damn good condition, too.'

'Good God!' James Westlake stared at him incredulously. 'Well, if it is, my fellow Trustees aren't likely to waste much time bothering about exactly how it turned up. I suppose there might be some legal complication, though...'

'Do you feel equal to taking over Miss

Escott?' Pollard asked, firmly bringing him back to the immediate present. 'As far as we're concerned, it's a case of a large-scale rethink, of course.'

'Most certainly, I'll look after her,' James Westlake replied, proceeding to get out of the car. 'This selling the house must be called off: it's complete nonsense. I'll deal with Moggs for her.'

Pollard accompanied him back into the building, suppressing a grin, and watched him advance, with hand outstretched, on an apprehensive Evelyn Escott.

'My dear,' he said to her, 'I hear you've made what may be a quite staggering discovery for RLSS. Heartless of me to want to see these stamps before commiserating with you over the wretched time you've been having, but it really is rather exciting. History possibly repeating itself, in fact.'

'First, the spectacular find of the Donne sonnet, and now this, in fact,' Pollard remarked, giving James Westlake full marks for tact as Evelyn Escott fumbled in the handbag she was clasping and extracted the small envelope. Toye helpfully produced a sheet of white paper, and half a dozen stamps were carefully laid out on it.

A couple of minutes later James Westlake

looked up from a careful scrutiny through a pocket lens.

'You're quite right, Super,' he said. 'This *is* a Mauritius twopenny blue. One fetched £15,000, or thereabouts, at auction recently. And this one here's a comparatively rare Hawaiian Missionary stamp... Well, I'm blessed!'

All four occupants of the room gazed reverently at the tiny, coloured rectangles on the sheet of paper. James Westlake picked up the envelope that had contained them, and turned it over. He gave an exclamation.

'There's something written on this. The ink's faded – we may have to use a violet lamp... Oh, thanks, Inspector. A bit of white paper inside may bring up the writing.'

He peered once again through his lens.

'Wait a bit. This is better. Old-fashioned handwriting with Greek e's... Property... Great heavens... Property of Evelyn Escott, Esquire! The old boy himself! He left his stamp collection to RLSS with his books, as you found out, my dear. I suppose for some reason he'd taken these out of his album, and died before putting them back. He went out at the drop of a hat, you know, Super.'

'Perhaps,' Pollard suggested, 'you and Miss Escott would like to discuss further this staggering piece of luck?'

James Westlake was instantly apologetic. 'Abominable to take up your time like this. Treasure trove just goes to one's head. There's quite a bit to discuss, you know,' he added, turning to Evelyn. 'I'd feel happier if this little lot were dropped into the night safe at the bank. Would you come along with me while we fix that, then back to my place for lunch?'

A few minutes later Pollard watched them go, Evelyn rendered slightly flustered and awkward by unaccustomed male attentiveness. Before leaving she had thanked him personally, with a warm sincerity he found touching, and had also spoken courteously to Toye.

'You miserable old truffle hound,' Pollard remarked amicably, as Toye closed the door behind the departing pair. 'Sniffing out improbable romances a mile off. I suppose it's dawned on you that, in spite of the lady's breathtaking disclosures, we're really no further on?'

Toye looked surprised. 'Well, *Y's* out of it,' he protested.

'Fair enough. But we knew all along that *Y* couldn't have been directly involved in Brown's death, whatever he or she was up to.

And we still don't know if Brown slipped and fell accidentally or was given a helping hand, do we? Let's reconstruct. Brown goes home and discovers that the packet of stamps isn't in her handbag. She assumes that it has fallen out and, on thinking back, decides that the most likely place for this to have happened is the yard at the Athenaeum, when she took her ignition key out of the bag. She hares back on foot to search for it... Why are you looking so ruddy disapproving?'

'The wheel marks in the gravel showed that she parked near the doors, nowhere near as far back as the boiler house,' Toye objected. 'So why should she go searching there, and notice that the door was open? If it was, that is.'

'Easy,' Pollard replied. 'The packet was very light and could have been blown down the yard. We don't know offhand what the weather was like at about half-past six on Wednesday evening; but it was cooking up for a filthy night, so there would almost certainly have been some wind. As to whether the boiler house door was open or not, well, just think yourself into *X's* skin. If we're right about his digging in in the boiler house, earlier on, he couldn't have known that Mrs

199

Habgood had opened the yard doors again after Brown had left. He'd picture them shut and assume that there was no risk of anyone's barging into the library from the yard. But there was always the chance of one of the Habgoods coming in from the hall or the flat: he probably wouldn't have known that Mr H. was out of action. *X's* instinct – the standard one for a breaker-in – would have been to have a quick, quiet getaway lined up. Remember that the yard doors have a Yale lock: he could get out through them fast enough.'

Toye reluctantly conceded these points.

'Well, then,' Pollard went on, 'the evidence points to Annabel Brown's discovering the open door, deciding that somebody is up to no good inside, and watching from behind the oil tank with blackmail in mind. After *X* has pushed off she goes in and searches under the librarian's table with her torch. She draws a blank but discovers the bust-open cupboard. Being an opportunist, she decides to cash in and help herself to some saleable first editions. And here we are again at the brick wall. What happened next?'

They sat in heavy silence for a couple of minutes. Finally Toye suggested that *X* might have returned for a second lot of books. Brown, on hearing him come in, would have crouched down in the gallery, and either been spotted or unwisely challenged him. He could have gone for her near the top of the staircase and scarpered after her fall. The door Ernie heard closing would have been the bookshelves swinging to after X had gone through.

Pollard agreed that this reconstruction was a possibility, but pointed out that X's return visit to the library would be a major hazard for the chap. Abbot's Green might be deserted on a winter evening but, if anyone did happen to be around, a bloke carrying a fairly heavy case of some sort would be noticeable – and probably remembered. Besides, where would he have dumped the first lot?

'Car,' Toye replied without hesitation. 'Parked somewhere near, all nice and handy.'

'I knew you'd say that. Cars and romance are your things, aren't they? No, but seriously, all this gives us something to work on. Now, then, I haven't had a chance to tell you about a conversation I had with Inspector Harris just now. I got some quite suggestive gen about Peter Escott...'

Toye listened, immobile and attentive.

'Of course, a case against the chap's pure

speculation at present,' Pollard concluded, 'but there are these pointers.'

'His knowing the building, and going up to the flat with the Professor,' Toye said thoughtfully. 'How would it have worked out for time, if he'd been up to funny business over the key?'

'It's exactly what the funny business could have added up to that's bothering me. Suppose he left the old boy doodling away in the Habgoods' sitting room, nicked the key, went back to the gallery and down the staircase. Well, as you'll remember, Westlake thought this just wasn't on. It's only his opinion, of course, but he knows how people react at these parties, and I'm inclined to give it a good deal of weight.'

They relapsed into silence. Pollard, frowning heavily, began to doodle a spiral staircase on a sheet of blotting paper. Quite suddenly an idea took shape in his mind with startling clarity.

'Damn it!' he shouted. 'Just how dim can you get? Escott needn't have gone back to the library at all! He could have left the flat by its front door, gone down the stairs into the hall, and out into Abbot's Green. The yard doors would have been open for people at the party to park inside. Escott only had to slip into the yard and unlock the boiler house door from the *outside*. Anybody seeing him coming or going through the main front door of the Athenaeum would simply think he was fetching something from his car, or had gone to put on a parking light, or whatever.'

'You've got it, sir,' Toye said, gazing at him with ungrudging admiration.

'About time, too, And if that's the way it was done, we've still got to find out how he got into the boiler house from the library, and unbolted the door on the inside. Of course, the fact that Evelyn Escott didn't notice him around on Wednesday isn't conclusive. She's obviously crazy about the place and this history she's writing, and could have been dead to the world outside her reference books. We'd better contact the other people who used the library during the day, even if Habgood's prepared to write them off.'

Toye, looking like a meditative owl, came up with a suggestion born of considerable experience of church socials.

'There's always the heck of a lot of clearing-up to do after one of these get-togethers,' he said with feeling. 'Could it be that this young Escott stayed behind to lend a hand, so that he could slip the bolt back then?'

Pollard stared at him.

'Neat,' he said. 'I wonder. From what Harris said about Escott, I should expect him to fade out at the first signs of a job to be done, but we can check up with Mrs Habgood. She'll have been directing operations. If you're right, it solves the problem of how Escott got in, of course. He could have turned up from the yard just a short time before five-thirty when the library closed, and the Habgoods or Annabel would shut the yard doors. Then he'd have waited quite a while, I think, to make sure that the library had been locked for the night. Hence the stacking chair drawn up to the boiler, leaving those helpful marks. But we've simply got to keep our eye on the ball and find out, first of all, if Escott left Professor Thornley for long enough on Tuesday evening to do that unlocking job. If he didn't, all these bright ideas about keys and bolts are just no go.'

'Ring the Professor?' Toye asked.

'Yeah. They'll have their members' addresses and telephone numbers round at the Athenaeum. Let's go.'

Chapter 9

Abbot's Green was an unexpected backwater off a busy street near the town centre of Ramsden. Originally, there had been a pleasant garden in the middle, exclusive to the residents. The national demand for scrap-iron in 1940 had uprooted the protective railings; now there was merely a dispirited area of rank grass and straggling shrubs, often ravaged by marauding children and haunted by stray cats. The houses, square and solid early nineteenth-century, stood on the outer side of the encircling road – the distinctive façade of the Athenaeum being diametrically opposite the entry to the Green from the street.

A preservation order had prevented architectural outrages, but the houses, like the former garden, had a forlorn air. The well-to-do families had all departed, driven out by the changing economic climate and the disappearance of domestic help. There had been a takeover by professional and business interests. Nearly all the houses were now in non-resident multiple occupation by doctors of consultant status, dentists, architects, insurance companies and others. The new landlords appeared to be more concerned with their rents than the maintenance of their properties, judging from patched roofs, flaking paintwork and derelict front gardens mainly in use as car ports.

'Dead as a doornail after working hours,' Pollard commented, as Toye drove slowly round towards the Athenaeum. 'Still, somebody might have been working late last Wednesday, and run into X or $A.N.$ *Other* when he came away. If X turns out to be young Escott, he might even have been recognized. I think it's worth asking Cook to put on a house-to-house inquiry.'

'There's the chap with the brief-case Ernie Dibble says he saw,' Toye said.

'Let's face it,' Pollard replied. 'If that chap was X and had done the break-in, he'd had nothing to do with Brown's fall. Ernie didn't hear the crash and the door closing until quite ten minutes later, by the time he'd got to the Athenaeum and messed around.'

'So we'd be back with Mrs Habgood as the only suspect?'

'This is it. And even if we unearth a motive, I don't see a hope in hell of charging her.'

'If we get X there's a fair chance of getting the books back,' Toye pointed out.

'Small beer, seeing we're down here to clear up a death under highly suspicious circumstances, old chap. Better than nothing, I suppose. Lord, what a stink it'll raise if X really is this Escott chap: great-great-grandson of the old boy they call their Founder in bated breath, as if he were the Almighty. Well, here we are. We ought to be on to Thornley soon, anyway.'

They were greeted by a complete change of atmosphere on going into the Athenaeum. The stuffy deadness had vanished in the bustle of a vigorous cleaning operation. The library door was propped open, and the whine of a vacuum cleaner and women's voices were audible within. There was a strong smell of furniture polish.

Pollard advanced on the office and looked through the glass panel of the door. Alastair Habgood was typing at his desk, surrounded by a confusion of papers and books that suggested a breakdown of normal routine. On catching sight of Pollard he beckoned him to come in, and began to lever himself up out of his chair.

'Don't get up on my account,' Pollard urged him. 'We're sorry to bother you when you're busy, but there's a bit of information you could give us quickly, I think: Professor Thornley's telephone number.'

With a fleeting look of surprise, Alastair Habgood pulled forward a small card index box.

'That's an easy one,' he said, flicking through the cards. 'All our members' addresses and telephone numbers are here. I'll jot it down for you.'

Pollard watched him shift his position and wondered if he were in pain. He certainly looked drawn and in some way mentally dislocated, as though unable to adjust to the sudden irruption of violence into his tranquil academic world. You'd expect a chap with his war experience to be tougher, Pollard thought. But it was a long time ago and he's managed to forget it. All this must be a beastly sort of resurrection.

'I suppose one doesn't ask if you're getting anywhere?' Alastair Habgood inquired tentatively, passing a slip of paper across.

'Thanks,' Pollard said, putting it into his wallet. 'One almost invariably does, you know, and gets a dusty answer. But I can't see any harm in telling you that we've at least cleared quite a bit of ground. And, by the way, we do realize how extremely unpleasant all this if for you, personally.'

'Decent of you to say that.' Alastair Habgood pushed the typewriter to one side and rested his folded arms on his desk. 'I feel so hideously responsible for this mess, you know. I mean, if Annabel was a wrong 'un, surely I ought to have spotted it? I've been damned casual about locking the gallery door into the flat, too. And then there's the loss of the books. The library's in my care and I've fallen down on that as well.'

Over-developed sense of responsibility, Pollard thought. Probably a hangover from the war, too. That's what getting him down. The possibility of his wife's being involved in Brown's death doesn't seem to have entered his head. He looked, with sympathy and liking, at the despondent figure in front of him.

'As we see it, you've nothing to reproach yourself with, Mr Habgood,' he said. 'And it's early days, you know. We've hopes of getting those books back. Meanwhile, it must be heavy going without an assistant. Any chance of some temporary help till you can find another?'

'I've had offers from several of our members, but explaining what wants doing, then checking up on the job afterwards, is really more bother than it's worth. I'll have to face it, though, once we reopen. By the way, that list of people at the party you wanted is nearly complete. I'm actually typing it now.'

Pollard thanked him. 'Can we have a word with Mrs Habgood before we go? Just an idea we'd like to put to her.'

'Certainly. She's getting the library straight with Clare, but they're nearly through. Come and have a look. You've never seen it in its normal state.'

Clear winter sunlight was filtering down from the domes. To Pollard the library seemed much larger and more colourful than on his earlier visits. It was bright with fresh flowers and newly-polished furniture.

As he came in with Toye, escorted by Alastair Habgood, Clare Fenner appeared from one of the bays with a duster in her hand, and smiled recognition. She went to Laura – who was hoovering the carpet, with her back to the door – and touched her on the shoulder. Laura turned her head, caught sight of the three men and for a brief moment went completely rigid. Against the formal background of books and portraits, the two women formed a striking picture: the one young and confident, the other bearing the imprint of life's exigencies and frozen in the grip of fear.

In less than a second the scene dissolved. Laura switched off the Hoover and came forward in the sudden silence, her normal brisk and cheerful self.

'So sorry,' she said. 'I didn't hear you come in. This thing makes such a row.'

Pollard apologized for arriving at an inconvenient time. 'We won't hold you up for more than a few minutes,' he told her. 'It's simply that we'd like you to give us as complete a picture as you can of the clearing-up on Tuesday night when the party was over. It may seem quite beside the point, but one can't have too much detailed background information in an inquiry of this sort.'

This time, he was quite sure that Laura Habgood relaxed at what was obviously an unexpected turn in the conversation.

'I'll do my best,' she said, 'though I can't imagine that anything we did is likely to interest you. Let's sit down, shall we?' she added, glancing in her husband's direction.

They all found seats and sat in an informal group, Clare perching on the arm of her uncle's chair. Nox, who had emerged from under the sofa when the Hoover was switched off, leapt on to his knee and began to knead it purposefully. Laura leaned back, making her characteristic gesture of trying to flatten her resilient hair.

'Now let me think.' She shut her eyes for a moment. 'Eight members stayed to help. Miss Escott and two other women collected up the remains of the eats and took them along to the kitchen. The little kitchenette down here, I mean, not ours upstairs. The men packed up the glasses – we hire from our wine merchant for parties – and the empties and the sale-or-return, unopened stuff. Various people got the heavy pieces of furniture back into their usual places. I remember being astonished at seeing Peter Escott rounding up the stacking chairs and putting them away in the store behind the *trompe-l'œil:* I've never known him lend a hand before, the young blighter.' She hesitated briefly. 'It seems rather offbeat to mention it after what's happened, but Annabel was hanging round him at once stage. Getting no change, though, and I think she must have decided to slope off. She certainly wasn't with the last lot of people I let out. That was at about half-past nine.'

'Thanks very much, Mrs Habgood,' Pollard said, carefully excluding any sign of satisfaction from his voice. 'That fills in our record nicely. Now we'll remove ourselves. I must say, the library's looking fine after all the hard work you and Miss Fenner have put in.'

'The Trustees are very keen for members to start coming in as usual tomorrow, aren't they, Alastair? We want everything to seem perfectly normal.'

'I'm surprised how our members seem to be taking it in their stride,' Alastair said. 'They're being awfully decent to us, too. Ringing up, sending flowers for Laura and asking us to meals. We had lunch with the Escotts yesterday, and young Peter took Clare out on Friday night to give her a break. Today we're due to lunch with the Chairman.'

Glancing at Clare Fenner's pleasant, rather serious face, Pollard had an uneasy qualm. What was the blighter's game, he wondered?

'I must say it's been a help not having to cook this morning,' Laura was saying. 'And you always get a super meal at Mr Westlake's.'

'You certainly mustn't be late for it, then,' Pollard replied, as he rose to leave.

His eyes fell on the Founder's portrait over the fireplace and he suddenly understood why Evelyn Escott's face had seemed familiar.

Once they were safely clear of the Athenaeum he turned to Toye. 'That idea of yours was a winner, old chap,' he said. 'All your humping of trestle tables and whatever after binges in your parish hall has paid off.'

Toye looked modestly gratified. 'You might say we're closing in on young Escott,' he replied cautiously, 'but it all hangs on what this Professor Thornley says. We're moving. I feel it in my bones. Towards pin-pointing X's identity. I mean, and as you said just now, possibly getting the books back. After that – full stop? Anyway, let's drive like hell to the police station, and we'll ring Oxford.'

On arrival they installed themselves in their room, and Pollard dialled Professor Thornley's home in North Oxford, with a satisfactory feeling of having arrived at the penultimate milestone of an exceedingly tedious journey. The persistent ringing tone was first a surprise, then an infuriating frustration. In reply to Toye's suggestion that the family might not have got back from church, he muttered an inappropriate remark under his breath. Finally, when he had all but given up hope, the ringing tone abruptly ceased.

'Who is it? What do you want?' demanded

214

an elderly female voice, so loud and raucous that he hastily moved the receiver several inches away from his ear.

'May I speak to Professor Thornley?' he asked, unconsciously raising his own voice.

'I'm not deaf, whoever you are,' replied the voice. 'No need to shout at me. Speak like a civilized being, can't you?'

'I – want – to – speak – to – Professor – Thornley,' Pollard enunciated clearly, moving to allow Toye to listen in.

'Well, you can't. My son's gone to a wedding in London. Won't be back till the last train tonight. They've all gone, and I'm not taking any messages.'

'I haven't asked you to,' Pollard replied, holding on to his temper with difficulty. 'Can you give me his telephone number in London?'

'No, I can't.'

'Did you say the Professor was returning by the last train *from London* tonight?'

'That's what I said. Can't you understand plain English?' The receiver was slammed down.

'Old cow!' Pollard exploded, with a reciprocal slam. He slumped down on his chair as Toye temperately remarked that elderly relatives could be a problem, and sat frowning into space for a full minute.

'Look here,' he said at last, 'I'd better go up. It's bound to be Paddington, and there won't be all that number of middle-aged couples on the last train to Oxford. I'll have the train times vetted at the Yard and get back here somehow. It'll be much more satisfactory to talk to Thornley face-to-face. And I can put in a report at the Yard and possibly have a word with the AC. Time he realized this job is a dead end. I might even get a couple of hours at home.'

Toye, scenting the possibility of making some inquiries on his own, encouraged this idea.

'I could nose round a bit here,' he suggested. 'See if I can pick up anything on Escott's car last Wednesday night, for instance.'

'If anybody can, you will,' Pollard said. 'Only I don't want the local chaps brought in on the Escott trail until Thornley's evidence is in the bag. No point in stirring up a hornet's nest unless it's a necessary. Here, run me to the station. There's a train to town in ten minutes.'

After satisfying himself that Pollard had managed to board the London train, Toye

216

drove to a car-park that he had previously marked down, then looked around for a pub. It was packed with Sunday lunchtime drinkers but he managed to make his way to the bar and get served. In a comparatively quiet corner, he planned his afternoon programme over beer and sandwiches, oblivious of the babel around him.

Half an hour later he returned to the car-park, having stopped on his way at a telephone kiosk. He learned from the directory that Colin Escott's private address was Hollacott House, Brinton, Ramsden. Sitting in the car, he consulted an Ordnance Survey map, found that Brinton was a small village four miles to the north of Ramsden and started off. A tentacle of new building including a housing estate extended along the road, but once clear of this he drove through open country until a church tower and a cluster of roofs appeared ahead. He slowed down, inspecting the outlying houses, and paused at a fashionable hanging sign on a post by an open drive gate. Hollacott House, he read. Deciding against parking at the side of the road, he drove on and found a space by the lych gate of the church. The village seemed completely deserted, and Toye concluded that the population was either still eating or sleeping off its Sunday dinner. At the same time he was probably being observed from behind curtains and ramparts of pot plants; it seemed advisable to behave like a tourist and visit the church. He spent about ten minutes on this, then emerged for a stroll round the village. Finally he sauntered off in the direction of Hollacott House, the view of his progress soon being cut off by an opportune bend in the road.

Toye stood in the gateway and prospected. A short drive curved round to the front of a house, which he correctly identified as a period piece which had had a packet spent on it. He noted the cream-washed walls, fresh paintwork and new thatch protected by fine-meshed wire netting. The drive was free of weeds and the bordering shrubs had been carefully pruned. Somewhere near there was a bonfire. Moving to one side, he saw what he had hoped to find: a large garage, joined to a side entrance to the house by a covered way, but out of sight of the front windows. Its doors were open and three cars stood inside, one of which was a sports model. That'll be the young chap's for sure, he thought, and began to make his way forward behind the shrubs bordering the drive, reaching the garage without crossing open ground.

It was stone built, and must have been a barn or something of the sort, he thought, as his eye fell on a ladder leading to an open trap door and a loft overhead. He took out his notebook and entered the makes and registration numbers of the three cars: a Triumph Stag, a BMW 1600 – probably a runabout for the lady of the house – and a TR4, bought secondhand, Toye thought. From what the Super said, the young chap wouldn't have had the cash for a newer model. He's looked after it, though: I'll grant him that...

A door opened with startling suddenness. Toye, who was capable of moving with a silent speed that had often surprised Pollard was up the ladder and into the loft before advancing footsteps arrived in the garage below. He dropped noiselessly to the floor and now wriggled as near to the open trap door as he dared. There was the unmistakable sound of a car's bonnet being opened: he risked a look. A young man in sweater and jeans was bent over the engine of the TR4. It seemed reasonable to assume that it was Peter Escott. As the young man straightened up, Toye hastily drew his head back. A metallic clatter suggested that a tool was being selected from among others.

The floor of the loft was uncomfortably hard and also dusty. Toye, always dapper in appearance, had gloomy thoughts about his suit, a fairly recent buy. How would dry cleaning look on his expense account for this trip, he speculated? Without warning, a catastrophic urge to sneeze engulfed him, and he gripped his nose savagely in a handkerchief, while cramming his left fist against his mouth. As the bonnet of the car was shut down, the paroxysm mercifully departed, as suddenly as it had developed. A moment later the door of the car was opened and the roof light came on. The engine roared into life and was revved up several times, apparently for test purposes. Toye risked another look and got a clear view of the young man, who was absorbed in interpreting the deafening noise. Apparently he was satisfied, as it ceased abruptly. For a few moments he sat motionless, gazing ahead, leaning his arms on the steering wheel; then suddenly dropping his head on to them, as if oblivious of his surroundings and deep in thought.

Toye estimated that two full minutes elapsed before there was a movement, and the young man sat up again and began to feel in the pocket of the driver's door. Toye caught his breath as he pulled out a pair of rubber gloves and looked at them for some seconds, then thrust them into the pocket of his duffle coat. Then, as if with sudden decision, he got out of the car.

The car door was slammed and there was the sound of departing footsteps, seeming to go round the back of the garage. Toye was down the ladder in a flash and stood tensely listening. There was a snapping of twigs, and he slipped out in time to see a figure disappearing towards what looked like a vegetable garden. The smell of a bonfire was stronger here, and Toye spotted a tenuous coil of smoke rising further ahead. With mounting excitement, he stalked his prey, in a manner of the heroes and villains of his favourite Westerns, and found cover behind a greenhouse.

A figure in a duffle coat was raking the bonfire with a stick. Toye's view through the greenhouse panes was distorted, but some object was being dragged out of a pocket and deposited on the embers. Further raking pulled the fire together again, and an armful of garden rubbish was thrown on to it. Finally, after watching it for several moments, the young man strode off in the direction of the house.

Toye watched him disappear and listened intently for the shutting of a door. After what seemed an hour he heard it, and ran to the bonfire, kicking at it vigorously. The gloves were degenerating into a sticky mess that gave off a revolting smell, but they were still partially intact. Enough left of the fingers to take dabs, Toye thought, heroically collecting the unpleasant remains in his clean handkerchief. Pausing only to re-assemble the fire as best he could, he beat a hastily retreat from cover to cover, until he safely reached the drive gate. Fortunately, no one witnessed his exit, but he could hear voices from beyond the curve of the road, and encountered a group of children with a mongrel dog, which rushed at him excitedly. It was called off in robust terms but the children stared at him curiously.

''E don't mean no 'arm,' one of them said. 'Bin after mushrooms, mister?'

Detecting a mocking undertone, Toye realized that he knew nothing of the life cycle of edible fungi and replied in a jocular tone that he had always heard Brinton was famous for mushrooms. Loud laughter greeted this sally, and he raised a hand in greeting and walked on. In the sanctuary of the Hillman, he transferred the handkerchief and its nauseous contents to a plastic box and started off for Ramsden, giving the children a friendly wave as he drove past them.

Back at the police station, he examined the gloves under a strong light and was delighted to find that one of the thumbs and two of the fingers were intact. He extracted the blown-up photographs of X's prints from the case file and cautiously took an impression from his find. The result was, beyond question, conclusive: Peter Escott was X.

Toye sat for a few moments in silent grati-fication. When you were teamed with a bril-liant chap like Pollard it sent you up to pull off something really worthwhile on your own. His training and methodical temper-ament then reasserted themselves. There was plenty left for him to do. If you were going to pull a bloke in, the more cut-and-dried evidence you had lined up, the better. There were Escott's movements on Wednes-day evening to look into, and the possibility of his car being parked somewhere near the Athenaeum. Toye carefully labelled the plastic box, put away the photographs and, after a refreshing cup of tea in the canteen, set out on foot.

He had made a mental note of the address

of the Escott firm; and ten minutes later was standing in front of a modern office block with an imposing entrance, surmounted by the words 'Escott House'. To the left of the main door, a brass plate was inscribed in flowing calligraphy, 'E. J. Escott'. So the old chap founded the estate agency, too, Toye thought. Eye to business as well as book learning and stamp collecting. He decided that Colin Escott had been behind the building of the block and was doing nicely out of rentals, as well as housing his own firm. Well below the brass plate were modest boards indicating other businesses accommodated in Escott House. He was on the point of walking to the Athenaeum to find out how long this would take, when he noticed a padlocked iron gate at the side of the building, and peered through it. It was a small car park, with spaces marked off by white lines, and presumably intended for users of Escott House. It occurred to him that it was probably locked each evening and that the timing of this might throw some light on Peter Escott's movements.

The street was empty, but about fifty yards further on Toye saw an illuminated pub sign, 'The Volunteer'. He looked at his watch: it was just on six o'clock, and he decided that it might be worth dropping in. He found the bar open and the landlord engaged in polishing glasses and disposed to chat. In the character of a Londoner visiting Ramsden on business, Toye began by being complimentary about modern developments in the town.

'Nice office block along the street,' he remarked, setting down a half-empty glass and leaning against the counter. 'Plenty of room inside but not so tall that it makes everything round about look squat.'

The landlord agreed that Escott's had done a good job over it. 'Got an architect down from London,' he added. 'There was feeling, but I don't say they weren't right.'

'Good idea having that space for parking cars at the back,' Toye went on. 'The street'd be choked with cars, else.'

'You're dead right. It's bad enough as 'tis. Traffic in the town gets worse every year, and what does the Council do about it?'

Before Toye could answer this rhetorical question, the door was pushed open and a small dark man came in, to be greeted by the landlord as Tom.

'Gentleman here's bin admirin' your place,' he told the newcomer, adding for Toye's benefit that Mr Billings here was caretaker over to Escott House.

Tom Billings was a voluble extrovert, and within minutes Toye was hearing how he was responsible for every blessed thing over there: maintenance, cleaners, the lot. The mere mention of the car park led to a diatribe on the efforts of the general public to sneak their cars in and leave 'em there for free, now that the Council had made the free parks into paying ones.

'I suppose you lock the place after office hours, or you'd be packed out till the pubs close?' Toye suggested.

Tom Billings described with gusto how he locked the gate on the stroke of a quarter to seven, Monday to Friday, having seen the cleaners out. It kept them on their toes, knowing they'd got to be out on time. He didn't wait for nobody. Then he walked down to the 'Volunteer' for his pint, regular as clockwork. The landlord, invited to testify to his customer's punctuality, agreed that you could set your watch by him.

'Of course the bosses 'as their own keys,' Tom Billings concluded. 'Week-ends, gate's kept locked, unless there's a delivery, that is.'

The bar was filling up. As soon as he decently could, Toye disengaged himself from the loquacious Tom Billings and returned to Escott House. Looking at his watch, he started to walk briskly, but not conspicuously fast, to the Athenaeum by the most direct route. Ernie Dibble, he reminded himself, had heard the clock on the parish Church strike seven *after* taking cover in the bushes. One couldn't be exact to a minute, but this must put the time of the crash of Annabel Brown's fall at between ten and five to seven. The boy had hung about in the hall before summoning up courage to run for it, and there had been an interval before he heard the clock.

As he walked, Toye turned these points over in his mind. On reaching the front door of the Athenaeum he looked at his watch again. He had been exactly fifteen minutes en route. He stood and thought. If it was Peter Escott who had closed the door quietly after Brown's fall, he would have arrived back at Escott House at between five- and ten-past seven. Billings would have been in the 'Volunteer', and the cleaners, however disposed to linger and chat, would certainly have cleared off. Still, it was something to have worked out this possible timing, and Cook's chaps might be able to get on to somebody who'd seen a chap carrying a case. Besides, in order to get home, Escott would have used his key to get his car out of the car park. A TR4 was the sort of car people noticed.

Wouldn't it have been easier, though, Toye argued with himself, to have parked the car near at hand? The door Ernie heard closing could have been Escott returning for a second lot of books, this time finding himself confronted by Brown, who'd come into the library from snooping behind the oil tank. So what? Did he find her hiding in the gallery, panic and give her a push? Or did he startle her, so that she took a hasty step in the dark and stumbled?

Feeling that he was straying into the dangerous realm of speculation, Toye set off to reconnoitre the neighbouring streets, and decided that there were plenty of places where a car could have been parked well away from a lamp.

Finally he began to retrace his steps towards the police station and the Hillman. His thoughts reverted to the debris of the rubber gloves with keen satisfaction. All that was needed now to pull young Escott in on the theft charge was the Professor's evidence that the chap had gone off and left him in the flat during the party for, say, five minutes. Plenty of time to get the boiler house door unlocked if you looked slippy.

Some hours earlier, Pollard had sprinted down the platform and boarded the London train by a flying leap. He found a seat and leant back in it to recover his breath. As the suburbs glided past and began to give place to fields and coppices, he recognized in himself a feeling of relief, even of exhilaration. He had experienced it on previous occasions when it had been possible to snatch a few hours away from the scene of a case. In earlier days he had felt like this at the beginning of a week-end *exeat* from his school.

He was sitting with his back to the engine, and as the train gathered momentum, Ramsden seemed to be receding rapidly but at the same time developing a sharp clarity, as if he were looking at it through powerful binoculars. The people with whom he was involved stood out distinctly. Perhaps because of his sensation of being rushed through the countryside at ever-increasing speed, they all seemed to be moving forward with an unshakeable purpose, oblivious of each other. On collision courses, Pollard thought...

Presently, it struck him that an unusual

number of these people were dominated by a ruling passion of one kind or another. There was Annabel Brown's ruthless and single-minded pursuit of security, financial and social, which had led her by a devious path to her death. Evelyn Escott's whole life had apparently been directed towards the single goal of making her mark in the Ramsden Literary and Scientific Society and so asserting her status in her native town. Defensive and compensating fanaticism had carried Flo Dibble through a life of hardship. Laura Habgood fulfilled her domestic responsibilities at the Athenaeum with a kind of conscious efficiency, activated, perhaps, by the non-academic woman's desire to count for something in a scholarly environment. Perhaps, too, by the desire to protect her invalid husband, to whom, in Pollard's opinion, she was over-protective. A pity there had been no children, he thought. And behind them all was Old Evelyn Escott, confidently bulldozing all obstacles to his founding of the Ramsden Literary and Scientific Society.

He continued to focus on Laura. Her obvious fear of himself must, of course, be connected with Annabel Brown's death. It suggested that Brown had been blackmailing her and that she was afraid both of the subject of the blackmail's coming out, and of Brown's hold over her being seen as a motive for the girl's murder. But what could this hold have been? Some sexual indiscretion in the past? The age gap between the two women made it unlikely that Brown could have uncovered anything in Laura's pre-Ramsden past. And Inspector Cook had been emphatic that no scandal of any sort had ever arisen in connection with the Habgoods. Laura was obviously passionately devoted to her husband. Could it possibly be that he was the one who had put a foot wrong, and that Brown was blackmailing her as the price of keeping quiet about it? From his impression of Alastair Habgood, Pollard felt that this was unlikely but he filed the idea in his mind for future consideration. It was a mistake to be too subtle, though. Brown might have got on to some small fiddle of Laura's over the catering, for instance.

The train roared hollowly over a bridge, and then resumed its steadily pulsating rhythm. At this comfortable distance from Ramsden and its tensions, one could view the case more dispassionately. Pollard recognized that – surprisingly, in view of his initial reactions – he was now more hooked than ever. Was it because the virtual impossibility of finding out what had happened to Annabel Brown at the last was arousing bulldog tenacity in him? Not altogether, he admitted to himself with discomfort. It was the conviction that the essential clue had at one moment been in his hands, and he had let it slip...

Suddenly, the ticket collector thrust open the door of the compartment and broke into these reflections. Pollard put his punched ticket back into his wallet and decided to go along to the buffet car for a snack. He found the crumbs and slopped liquid on the tables so off-putting that he had a hasty sandwich standing at the bar, and then went back to his compartment. He would just about have time to put together an interim report for his Assistant Commissioner before getting in.

Later, on reading it through, he thought he could detect undertones of annoyance at having his leave postponed, and wondered how near the wind he could risk sailing. Then, with a grimace, he stuffed the sheets into his brief-case, and saw that the train was running into Paddington.

Almost as if echoing his thoughts on the Habgoods, he found the reports on them that he had asked for awaiting him. He studied them with interest but they were unilluminating. Both Alastair and Laura had come from middleclass homes and had had a grammar school education. Alastair, the elder by five years, had been allowed to sit for his FLA before call-up, subsequently serving with distinction in the Italian campaign, being invalided out in 1944. Laura Marsh had gone straight into the Wrens from school. Her war record had been creditable and on demobilization she had married Alastair, in 1946. At this time, he had a post in a city library in the Midlands and they had moved to Ramsden on his appointment as Librarian at the Athenaeum. That was all there was to it.

Pollard put the reports aside and inspected the documents set out on his desk. The pull of home was almost irresistible, but there were really urgent matters needing his attention. He reluctantly buzzed for his secretary and got down to work. They had almost cleared the most pressing backlog when a message came over the intercom demanding his presence in his Assistant Commissioner's office. Smothering an imprecation, he snatched up the Ramsden file and dashed out of the room.

The AC contemplated him quizzically, and indicated a chair.

'So, according to you, the answer is a lemon?' he opened, tapping the brief report in front of him.

Pollard sat down. 'I don't see any other solution, sir,' he said impassively, correctly interpreting this verbal shorthand.

The AC tilted his chair back, looking amused. 'I'm inclined to agree – on paper, so to speak. At the same time, disregarding the fact that you hate my guts at the moment for postponing your leave, and handing you a case unlikely to boost your inflated reputation still further, something's biting you, isn't it?'

'I suppose you might say so, sir,' Pollard admitted guardedly.

'I *am* saying so. Stop being bloody-minded, Pollard, and discuss the case rationally.'

Pollard, never able to stand out for long against the AC's barbed perceptiveness, looked at him and grinned.

'Sorry, sir. The fact is, I'm not really satisfied with the rational approach. I've got a hunch that I've missed something vital, but God only knows what. Toye and I have gone over the known facts till we're dead stale on them.'

'Where's Toye at this moment?'

'Down at Ramsden, sir, working on Peter Escott's movements last Wednesday night.'

The AC grunted and lapsed into silence.

'I'm satisfied with the way you're handling the inquiry,' he said at last, dropping his bantering tone. 'Perfectly sound to amass all the data about this young Escott before bringing a burglary charge. As you say, he might possibly crack and admit having had a struggle with the girl. Don't let yourself be distracted by wondering what to do next if he can prove he was clear of the place before the boy heard the crash. And go home for a breather before you meet this Professor johnny: you've got several hours in hand. How's the family?'

'The twins have got chicken-pox,' Pollard told him.

'Filthy complaint, especially when the scabs start dropping off all over the place. I hope to God you won't pick up shingles, Pollard. You could be off for weeks.'

Heartened by the implied compliment in this final remark, Pollard returned to his room. Within ten minutes he had rung Jane and was on his way home.

As he pushed open the front door of the house, the twins erupted from the kitchen in

235

their dressing gowns.

'Daddy!' Andrew yelled, 'Rose has got hundreds and hundreds of spots! I only had five!'

'Every bit of me's spotty, Daddy,' Rose assured him.

'Coming!' Jane called down from upstairs. 'I thought the best thing was to get their baths and supper over!'

Family life closed over Pollard's head.

Two hours later, sitting with Jane at the kitchen table after a leisurely meal, he stretched and looked at his watch. 'I needn't push off for another twenty minutes,' he said.

'Tell me,' Jane asked, 'when did you begin to feel that this vital clue had slipped past you?'

'This is it. I'm not sure. Quite early on. I'd seen the Habgoods for the first time, and vetted the shop, I think. Then I had a night-mare about it: a beastly one. I was just catch-ing up on the blasted clue when something unspecified and catastrophic happened to me – just as I woke up, all sweaty.'

Jane gave him a quick, unhappy look. 'Don't! Tom, it isn't a – a violent sort of case, surely?'

'Not in the least,' he reassured her. 'Forget the nightmare. It was obviously indigestion.

The Castle Hotel food is the good, solid type.'

'Much more likely to have been subconscious rat-race worry. How I hate the publicity racket,' she added vehemently.

'Come again,' he invited.

'I mean that you've been so conditioned by your success story that when you get a no-go case, you feel you're falling behind by not–'

'Hitting the headlines?' he chanted. 'You're so sharp you'll cut yourself one day, darling. In self-defence, pay and prospects do come into it, you know.'

'Listen,' Jane said. 'We've often talked about my going back to work, and something turned up a couple of days ago. It got round to the Inner Surrey College of Art that the twins are starting full-time school next term, and they've offered me a couple of half-days to start with. More in September if I want it... Lovely lolly coming into the house... Don't look so startled. You haven't been permanently conditioned into being our Universal Provider, have you?'

'A lot of my age group still fancy themselves in the part, you know. You're quite sure you want to go back to teaching, and that you can carry it without killing yourself!'

'Have lots of surplus energy. Will cope… So do I take it that we embark on the next phase of our married life?'

Pollard grinned at her. 'Yeah, it looks like it. I'll soon acclimatize. I'm a conservative type – small c.'

Jane rested her head on her hand, studying him critically.

'True,' she said. 'The odd thing is that you're basically newsworthy, too. I don't know why it is but some people are like lightning conductors where publicity's concerned. Honestly, you needn't bother about your image.'

'If I hit the bloody headlines over the case of the late Annabel Brown, love,' Pollard told her, getting up from the table, 'we'll rustle up a babysitter and have the night out of a lifetime in the West End. Hell! I must run for it!'

'I'll hold you to that night out,' Jane said, muffled in his hasty embrace.

Paddington was cavernous and echoing, its lights haloed in mist. The Oxford train was standing at its departure platform. Pollard walked its length twice, and satisfied himself that none of the passengers already sitting in it was Professor Thornley. He continued to stroll up and down, keeping an eye on the barrier, his shoulders hunched against the cold.

He felt revitalized and relaxed. One simply took the obvious next step and let the outcome decide the following. As the minutes went by, however, he began to hope fervently that Professor Thornley would not run it too fine. It would be the absolute end to have to travel down to Oxford with him and then somehow get back to Ramsden.

At last a group of people, with an indefinably festive air, came through the barrier. Wedding guests, Pollard thought instantly, and went forward. The next moment he raised his hat to a short man with rimless spectacles, wearing a tweed overcoat and incongruous woollen cap.

'Excuse me, sir,' he said, proffering his official card, 'are you Professor Thornley?'

As he spoke, Pollard was conscious of interest tinged with hilarity on the part of the younger members of the group. 'Coo, it's the fuzz!' a voice remarked audibly. 'What's Gramp been up to?'

A pair of sharp and humorous eyes behind the rimless spectacles were raised to Pollard's. 'Yes, I'm Thornley. What can I do for you? Go along and set some seats, the rest of you.'

Pollard stated his connection with the inquiry into Annabel Brown's death in the Athenaeum library at Ramsden.

'Yes, I've read about it,' the Professor replied. 'Where do I come in?'

'We understand, sir, that in the course of the party held in the library last Tuesday evening, you were taken up to the librarian's flat to see the ornamental plasterwork of the ceilings. Is this correct?'

'It is. So what, as the modern young say?'

'Would you state, as accurately as you can, all that you can remember about the time you spent there?'

'Certainly. A young man called Peter Escott took me up, having been humiliated beyond endurance by the inanities of his parents, who had been introduced to me. He was a young puppy, but reasonably well informed on the history of the building and the plaster moulding of the ceilings. I found the latter interesting, and he offered to get me a pamphlet about them from the office. In his absence, I sketched a few of the *motifs*. He returned, apologetically, having been unable to find a copy of the said pamphlet. Shortly afterwards, we returned to the library together. Another member of the Escott

240

family was engaged in showing other guests the ceilings while I was up there, a lady.'

'How long was Mr Escott absent while you were sketching, sir?' Pollard asked.

Professor Thornley gave him a long and very hard look.

'It is difficult to be exact, Superintendent, but certainly not less than five minutes. Seven or eight would be nearer the mark, I think.'

Chapter 10

Monday was ushered in by a false dawn in the small hours. Pollard got stiffly out of the train at Ramsden and gave up his ticket to a porter, who was manhandling milk churns and looked at him curiously. He walked down the deserted platform, his steps echoing. In the station yard he was confronted by Toye, against the background of the Hillman.

'What on earth do you think you're doing?' Pollard demanded. 'The hotel's only a bare five minutes from here. You ought to have turned in.'

Toye remarked, incontrovertibly, that the car was there to be used. He added that he had had a nice bit of shut-eye in the TV lounge; and that the night porter would have a pot of tea lined up when they got in.

'All in order,' Pollard told him as they moved off. 'Professor Thornley's prepared to state on oath that Escott was out of the flat for not less than five minutes. He finally put it at seven or eight.'

'That idea of yours about the boiler house being unlocked from outside was a winner, sir,' Toye observed.

'I ought to have got on to it a lot sooner. It's quite extraordinary how slow one can be to cotton on to the obvious. What have you got up your sleeve? You're positively sleek.'

'I managed,' Toye said demurely, 'to take possession of *X's* gloves.'

'Good God! Do you mean the ones he used for the break-in?'

'That's it. Rubber ones. The dabs have been checked up.'

'Can it be that you've spent my absence in breaking and entering?'

'In a manner of speaking,' Toye admitted, carefully negotiating the entrance to the hotel car park, 'you might say that I have.'

'You're not fit to be left on your own. Lead me to that pot of tea: you can come clean before I'm asleep on my feet.'

The day got off to a second start at half past seven, when a prearranged ring on the house telephone jerked Pollard into reluctant consciousness. Half an hour later, in the middle of a monosyllabic breakfast with Toye, he was summoned to take another call. As he dodged past waitresses carrying loaded

244

trays, a string of possible callers ran through his mind, Jane among them.

'Pollard speaking,' he said, on taking up the receiver.

Someone he had not thought of was at the other end.

'Habgood here. I hope it's all right to ring you at your hotel?'

'Perfectly OK, Mr Habgood. Go ahead.'

'The books have turned up. They've been dumped in one of our dustbins.'

Pollard wondered fleetingly why he had not given more consideration to this possibility. He assessed its implications while asking the obvious questions. He learned that the books were parcelled up in some sort of cellophane, and had been discovered by Clare Fenner about ten minutes ago, when she was taking out some rubbish to the bins in the yard.

'Nothing's been touched, I hope?' he asked.

'Nothing. Clare put the lid on again and came to tell me. She slammed the doors. Nobody can get in.'

'Fine,' Pollard said. 'We'll be right along.'

Back in the dining room, he briefed Toye, while gulping down the remains of his coffee. Five minutes later, they were driving out of the hotel car park.

Alastair Habgood was hovering on the threshold of his office as they walked into the Athenaeum: he was looking, as Pollard afterwards remarked to Toye, several years younger.

'Clare thinks there are about eight books there,' he told them, without preamble, 'so the whole lot may have been brought back. I hope to God they aren't damaged, especially the Chairman's *History of Glintshire*. It's in manuscript. I've got the key here,' he added, with barely concealed impatience.

'I expect they've been taken care of for the sake of their market value,' Pollard said, as they went out.

The yard doors showed no sign of forced entry or of having been recently sealed. The loose gravel immediately inside was trodden and scattered by the frequent passage of people and cars, and he realized that there would be no useful impressions here like the ones behind the oil tank.

'It's the dustbin on the right,' Alastair Habgood prompted.

Toye eased off the galvanised iron lid by its rim: Pollard looked down at the package of books resting on a roughly folded sack.

'Don't you use this bin?' he asked. 'There

doesn't seem to be any rubbish in it.'

'It's the one we keep for waste paper. We put it in the sack, and the collectors tip it out into a separate part of the van. They collect at about eleven on Wednesday mornings. My wife says no paper's been thrown out since. We haven't been functioning normally since all this happened, you see.'

At Pollard's suggestion, he and Toye lifted the dustbin by its side handles and carried it round to the office. He then rang the police station and asked for a fingerprint expert to be sent round.

'They'll get someone along at once,' he said, putting down the receiver and turning to the others. 'Meanwhile, I'd like to see Mrs Habgood and Miss Fenner. Toye, would you stay and get the chap started when he turns up?'

Alastair Habgood reluctantly detached himself from the books and led the way upstairs. Laura and Clare left their household chores and joined them in the sitting room. There was a general atmosphere of relief. Clare looked happy and excited. Nothing, Pollard thought, could make it clearer that Annabel Brown had been an alien element in the Athenaeum set-up. She had never belonged: beyond the passing inconvenience of the loss of her services, she would neither be missed nor regretted.

'I take it,' he said, addressing himself to the matter in hand, 'that your cleaner isn't here this morning?'

'No, she isn't, much against her will,' Laura replied. 'She has to go to court with her boy this morning – the one who robbed Miss Escott, so I told her not to think of coming to work, poor little thing. She was so upset. I had to promise her to polish the brass handle of the front door, myself: it's her pride and joy.'

'So that's how I came to be coping with the rubbish,' Clare put in.

Pollard smiled at her. 'And made the find of the year, didn't you? Now, what I want to check on is the last time anyone from this household went to that dustbin.'

Laura Habgood looked at him with a hopeless little shrug. 'I'm afraid,' she said, 'that nobody has opened it since last Wednesday morning's collection. It's like this. Flo Dibble's last job each day is to take the rubbish out – ours, from up here, and the stuff from the public rooms. Last Thursday morning she never got that far, of course, and hasn't been here since, as the place was closed. And Clare and I are quite

248

certain that we haven't taken out any waste paper. Most of it comes from the office, and my husband hasn't been doing his normal work.'

'Wasn't there any from the library when you cleaned it yesterday?' Pollard asked.

'Only a few scraps your people must have dropped into the baskets. It didn't seem worth taking out so little, so I tipped it into the office basket, to deal with this morning. We've been to the other bin several times, with household waste and dead flowers. It couldn't be more unhelpful, I'm afraid.'

'Well, we'll try another tack,' Pollard said. 'Access to the yard. Is it possible to work out when the doors have been standing open?'

'Starting on Wednesday evening,' Alastair said, after a pause, 'they must have been open until Annabel took her car out at about twenty to six and again from – say – a quarter to, until after Clare had arrived soon after seven. Then they blew open sometime during the night. Did either of you hear them?'

Laura and Clare shook their heads.

'We were all so rattled on Thursday morning that I never thought about them until Inspector Cook said he'd shut them, and

they mustn't be opened until further notice,'
Laura said. 'They stayed shut until after
supper on Friday. You remember you said it
didn't matter any more, just before you left.'

'I'm kicking myself in retrospect,' Pollard
replied. 'Can you draw up any sort of time-
table for the week-end?'

After some discussion one was put
together, and taken down by Toye, who had
joined them.

Day – Friday
Doors Open – About 8.0–10.30 pm
Whereabouts of Household – Visit to
friends (Rev. J. and Mrs Masters at Rectory).

Day – Saturday
Doors Open – About 9.30 am–3.30 pm
Whereabouts of Household – Morning
shopping. Lunch with Mr and Mrs Colin
Escott.

Day – Sunday
Doors Open – About 10.30 am–4.0 pm
Whereabouts of Household – Morning
cleaning of library. Dead flowers, etc. taken
out. Lunch with Mr Westlake.

Pollard took Toye's notebook and studied

the times.

'It looks wide open at first,' he said, 'but I'm pretty sure we can narrow it down. You see, anyone on foot, or even on a bicycle, would be noticeable if he was toting around that bundle of books, and cars are likely to be remembered. I can't see anybody turning up at intervals on the chance that the doors might be open. Did you mention your week-end plans to anyone?'

The Habgoods agreed that they had told the Rector and his wife about their lunch invitations.

'I suppose it's possible they passed it on,' Alastair said. 'But it would only have been to mutual friends.'

'We didn't tell the Escotts that we were going over to Mr Westlake's on Sunday, though,' Laura reminded him.

'Why not?' Pollard asked. 'Prearranged silence on the subject for some reason?'

'Well, yes,' Alastair replied. 'Colin Escott is one of the Trustees, and he and Mr Westlake don't always see eye to eye. Also, I'm an employee, and it isn't good policy to appear on too intimate terms with one's Chairman, you know.'

Clare Fenner cut into the conversation so abruptly that Pollard glanced at her in surprise. The happiness in her face had vanished, and she looked worried. 'Excuse me,' she said hurriedly, 'hadn't I better go and open up downstairs, if I'm not needed here any longer? It's just on ten.'

She coloured up as she spoke. The incident struck Pollard as oddly out of character.

'May she go?' Alastair asked him. 'We're anxious to get the place ticking over normally this morning.'

'By all means,' Pollard said, 'and I needn't keep Mrs Habgood any longer, either. Thanks for all your help, both of you. Shall we go back to the office and see how the finger printing's going?'

Clare had already slipped out of the room.

'Let Clare have your latchkey to the flat, Alastair,' Laura said as they got up. 'I want to go out and get the shopping done early. You run into fewer people.'

In the office they found Detective-Constable Neale, pink and enthusiastic; they examined the results of his work.

'Lovely dabs, sir,' he told Pollard. 'Beauties under the handle on top of the lid, where the chap had lifted it, and the same ones on the package. That shiny wrapping's taken them a treat. Rubber gloves, he was wearing.'

Pollard glanced inquiringly at Toye, who

nodded. '*X*'s all right, I'd say, sir. Of course we'll be checking up at the station,' he added hastily.

'Nice job, Neale,' Pollard said later, as the young detective finished his tests. 'We'll have to hang on to the books for a bit, I'm afraid, Mr Habgood, but I'll be personally responsible for seeing they're kept under proper conditions. Inspector, make out a receipt for them, will you?'

As he spoke, out of the corner of his eye he caught sight of a figure vanishing into the library. A possible, if astonishing, solution to Clare Fenner's recent behaviour suddenly flashed into his mind. Telling Neale to parcel up the books again, he left the office and went into the library himself. It was apparently empty. He stood for a few moments in front of the fireplace, contemplating old Evelyn's portrait. Then he turned and faced the room.

'Are you in here, Miss Fenner?' he called.

The silence that followed was marginally excessive. There was a slight sound, then she emerged from a bay, looking flushed and guilty.

'Did you want me, Mr Pollard?' she asked, with forced brightness.

'Yes, Miss Fenner,' he said. 'I want to ask

you a couple of questions. When you lunched with Mr and Mrs Escott on Saturday, was their son Peter one of the party?'

He watched her realize that anything but the truth would be futile.

'Yes, he was,' she replied, with an attempt to sound surprised.

'And did you tell him that you and Mr and Mrs Habgood were going over to lunch with Mr Westlake yesterday, either then or when you were out with him on Friday evening?'

As she hesitated, a young man in corduroy trousers and a polo-necked sweater walked out of the bay from which she had just come, and stood beside her.

'Yes, she did,' he said briefly. 'OK, I nicked the bloody books and I put 'em in the dustbin yesterday, when everybody was out. But if you think I pushed Annabel Lucas – Brown – down that contraption over there, you're wrong. I never set eyes on her.'

There was a short tense pause.

'We must ask you to come with us to the police station, Mr Escott,' Pollard said, 'and answer a number of questions.'

Peter Escott declined to send for a solicitor. 'Not unless you're going to charge me with manslaughter or murder,' he said, folding his arms and staring steadily across the table at Pollard, 'neither of which I've committed, as it happens.'

Pollard, meeting his challenging but wary eyes, recognized the likeness to old Evelyn. This lad's got brains, too, he thought, but no real purpose in life. Partly the times we live in, of course...

'Whether we finally decide to charge you, Mr Escott,' he said, 'depends on the account you give of your activities on Tuesday and Wednesday nights of last week, and if you can substantiate it. I suggest that you begin on it now.'

Peter Escott, who had blinked at the mention of Tuesday, considered, 'Not on,' he said. 'It's up to you to make the going.'

'As you like it. We'll begin with the centenary party at the Athenaeum last Tuesday evening, when you took Professor Thornley up to the Habgoods' flat to look at the ceilings.'

Peter Escott lowered his eyes and studied the table.

'We have evidence,' Pollard went on, 'that this visit to the flat was at your suggestion. As it was essential to Wednesday's break-in, no doubt you had other pretexts for going there, in case Professor Thornley turned down the idea.'

'Not true. Taking him up there just came into my head as a way of getting him away from my parents, who were making asses of themselves. I was getting hot under the collar.'

'So when did the idea of borrowing the key of the boiler house, and all that followed, come into your mind?'

'When we were looking at the ceiling in the Habgoods' bedroom and I spotted the key board behind the door.'

'You say that the whole elaborate plan for getting into the library and stealing the books occurred to you for the first time at that precise moment?' Pollard asked sarcastically. 'You're a quick thinker, Mr Escott.'

With a sudden convulsive movement, Peter Escott shifted his position.

'I didn't say anything of the sort. You're twisting things, the way the police always do. What I mean is that I've often thought it would be a good giggle to stir up the whole damn show. The blah that goes on about this potty little provincial hobbies club my great-great-grandfather founded, under an idiotic pretentious name, makes me sick. Anyway, the Athenaeum and everything in it ought to belong to us. He'd no right to chuck away family money like that.'

'You don't seem to be a very clear thinker,' Pollard remarked. 'You were annoyed with your parents for not sharing Professor Thornley's view of the Ramsden Literary and Scientific Society, yet, at the same time, write it off as a potty little provincial hobbies club. However, we'll let that pass. Having been suddenly inspired by the sight of the key board, what did you do next?'

Peter Escott relapsed into sullen silence.

'Very well, I'll tell you,' Pollard said. 'As Founder's kin, you no doubt know the building well. Professor Thornley's wish to make some sketches made it easy to leave him in the sitting room while you went off on the pretext of looking for a pamphlet for him. You took the key, went out of the flat and the front door, through the yard – which was open for car parking – and unlocked the door of the boiler house. In a couple of minutes or so you were back again, replaced the key, and reappeared in the sitting room, saying that you had unfortunately not been able to get hold of a copy of the pamphlet. It was quite simple to unbolt the door on the inside. You merely stayed behind – rather uncharacteristically, it seems – to help clear up the library after the party. You dealt with the stacking chairs, and slipped through to the boiler house from the storage space where they are kept.'

Pollard paused. Peter Escott had reverted to staring at the table, but the nervous flicker of his eyelids showed his mounting tension.

'We now have an interval until five o'clock on Wednesday evening,' Pollard resumed. 'It gave you plenty of time to work out your plan in detail. Your firm's office closes at five. You knew that the yard doors would be open until five-thirty, when Annabel Brown left in her car. You had ample time to get to the Athenaeum and into the boiler house from the yard. In fact, there was time to fill in until you felt it was safe to start breaking open the cupboard where the valuable books are kept. There was no point in being uncomfortable, so you took one of the stacking chairs and settled down by the boiler.'

This small domestic detail had the effect of making Peter Escott violently thrust back his chair and half rise to his feet. Almost simultaneously Toye was at the door, with his back to it.

'Sit down,' Pollard ordered brusquely. 'Do you admit these facts I've stated?'

Peter Escott subsided slowly and wiped his forehead with the back of his hand.

'Yes,' he said hoarsely, 'though God only knows how you've found it out. 'It's – it's what happened next you'll never believe.'

'I'm prepared to listen. Don't waste my time with a pack of lies, though.'

By means of a series of questions, Pollard went on to establish that Peter Escott had waited in the boiler house until six o'clock before moving. By this time, he judged that neither of the Habgoods was likely to come into the library again that night. He did not know that Alastair was in bed, nor that the yard doors had been reopened, and had no anxiety about anyone discovering that the door of the boiler house was unlocked. He opened it a little, on the unlikely chance of having to leave quickly, and went up the spiral staircase to the gallery. Forcing the lock of the cupboard proved much more difficult than he had expected. He was handicapped by having to work by the light of an electric torch and by fear of making a noise that might penetrate to the flat. Eventually he managed it, and selected eight books.

'Why didn't you tidy things up instead of leaving the cupboard wide open?' Pollard asked.

Peter Escott, now very white, replied that

he had thought he heard a movement down-stairs.

'I waited a bit, then decided to scram, using as little light as possible.'

'Did you see anyone or hear any more?'

'No.'

'Were you surprised to find the yard doors open?'

'I was scared stiff,' Peter Escott replied with feeling. 'I felt sure somebody was about and could have seen me. There's a beastly street lamp just outside.'

'What time was it?'

'God, I don't know. I was much too het up to bother about the time.'

The timing's vital, Pollard thought. This noise could have been Brown arriving about half-past six. If he's the chap Ernie saw making off about five minutes later, we can wash him out...

'Where was your car all this time?' he asked.

'In the office car park. All I wanted to do was to get back to it and clear off home.'

'Did you notice what time it was when you did get back to it?'

'Just on seven.'

Then he surely couldn't have been Ernie's chap, Pollard thought. He couldn't have taken twenty-five minutes to do a fifteen-minute walk, especially if he was stepping out. He proceeded to question Peter Escott minutely on the exact route he had taken, and became more and more convinced that he was not getting the whole truth.

'You're obviously lying,' he rapped out. 'You didn't go straight from door to door. Where else did you go?'

Finally Peter Escott admitted, with embarrassment, to having hidden in the garden of one of the Abbot's Green houses, in the hopes of shaking off anybody who might be following him.

'Did you see anyone?' Pollard demanded.

'Nobody came along after me, so I got going again after a bit.'

The story aroused Pollard's suspicions. Was it an attempt to account for time actually spent in the library with Annabel Brown? But a later departure from the Athenaeum would have meant a later arrival at Escott House. He questioned further but Peter Escott stuck to his statement that he had arrived there just before seven. Several clocks had struck the hour as he got to his car.

'What time did you get home?'

Peter Escott eyed him uneasily.

261

'Twenty-five-past seven.'

'In a TR4?' Pollard exclaimed incredulously.

'She wouldn't start at first ... her plugs were dirty.'

'Have you a witness to your return home?' Pollard inquired.

'Everybody was out. I can't prove it, if that's what you want.'

'Very well. Are there any witnesses to the time you arrived at Escott House?'

'Of course there aren't!' Peter Escott suddenly shouted. 'There's nobody there at that hour. And I didn't meet anybody I knew, either. Making it easy for you to prove I'm a murderer, isn't it?'

'What we're trying to do,' Pollard replied, 'is to get at the truth about the time when you left the Athenaeum. You see, we know the time of Annabel Brown's fall...'

'He refused to contact his people, or the office,' Pollard told Superintendent Daly and Inspector Cook. 'He's supposed to be inspecting a country property, so his absence won't raise any questions. We've left him putting a statement of his movements on Wednesday evening into writing.'

'Well, we're spared Colin Escott coming

round like a roaring lion for the moment,' Daly replied, looking worried. 'Gives us a chance to check up on any patrols who might have seen the chap going through the streets or on the road home. What do you make of him?'

'I'm not sure,' Pollard said slowly. 'The fact that he swears he left the Athenaeum in time to hang about, then still arrive at Escott House by seven, does suggest that he knows the time when Brown fell down the staircase – and is trying to prove he wasn't there. He's undoubtedly got some brains. On the other hand, bits of his statement do tie up with things we accept: Brown's arrival, for instance, and the chap with the brief-case Ernie saw. And Toye says he did clean the plugs of his TR4 on Sunday afternoon. One reliable bit of corroborative evidence would settle the whole business. Let's hope your people get on to something. Have you got on to Mr Westlake yet about the books?'

'Yeah. We asked him to come along and identify the one that's his. He'll be bowled over when he knows young Escott's in it up to the neck. He's always been hooked on the Ramsden Literary and Scientific set-up, and of course the Escott family's been in on it ever since the old chap founded it, just a hundred years back. That his car coming into the park, Cook?'

James Westlake came striding in triumphantly to recover his property, but the sight of the three men who looked up at him brought him to a sudden halt.

'What's up?' he demanded.

Pollard told him.

James Westlake sank on to a chair, utterly appalled. 'This is a God-awful mess,' he said. 'Do his people know?'

'No. He's supposed to be in the country, on the firm's business, and refuses to contact them. We picked him up at the Athenaeum, where he admitted to the break-in and the theft. He said he did it for a giggle. A protest, too, we gathered. He seems allergic to your Society. He could have meant to flog the books, of course, but I doubt if he's got the know-how.'

James Westlake exploded in fury. Recovering himself, he listened to an account of the efforts being made to check Peter Escott's statements.

'One can only hope to God he can anyway be cleared of anything to do with the girl's death,' he said. 'Wretched young waster that he is, I can't believe that he deliberately threw her downstairs... The appalling scandal for his family...'

He relapsed into silence and sat thinking, almost audibly.

'About the books,' Pollard said, after a lengthy pause. 'Since they've been returned I suppose prosecution isn't a foregone conclusion?'

'I'm thinking along those lines myself,' James Westlake replied, exchanging a glance with Superintendent Daly. 'It's partly a matter for my fellow-trustees, of course.'

Not for the first time, Pollard was amused by official reluctance to become embroiled with prominent local citizens. However, more serious matters were involved than a mere theft of books. Shortly afterwards, he left the others and returned to his room, wondering if the inquiries Toye was making at Escott House were achieving anything. In the light of the caretaker's clock-watching habits, the prospects seemed hardly hopeful.

Presently Peter Escott's written statement was brought in to him. He read it attentively several times, and admitted that it was concise, clear and identical with what had emerged at the interview. Putting it down, he reflected that you could combine intelligence with immaturity to an astonishing degree. The chap was unusually small-scale for his generation: kicking against his personal circumstances instead of campaigning against nuclear weapons or apartheid. I hope, he thought, that nice Clare Fenner hasn't fallen for him: she's worth twenty of him. I'm certain she went back into the flat, when we'd all cleared out, and rang him to come over at once. What exactly was going on between them when I barged into the library? Was she giving him a friendly tip-off that we were on his tail, or advising him to come clean?

The arrival of Toye, neat and impressive as always, cut short these speculations. Pollard looked at him inquiringly.

'Not much to report, I'm afraid, sir,' he said. 'Tom Billings, the caretaker, can swear that Escott's TR4 was in the park when he locked up at quarter to seven, and that it had gone when he came back to his supper at eight o'clock. He and his wife have a flat at the top of the building, but she doesn't remember hearing it go out. The only other thing I got was the names and addresses of the cleaners. Billings said he'd booted them out as usual at quarter to seven. There are three of them, and I've been round to see two, who'd nothing to tell me. They'd gone straight home. The third, funnily enough, is Mrs Dibble. I couldn't get hold of her, of course, as she's in court with Ernie. But Billings did say he'd had a breeze with her, Wednesday night. Something about her not being finished in time and wanting to stay on, but he wasn't having any.'

Pollard looked up from doodling a spiral staircase on a piece of blotting paper. 'She'd hardly have sneaked back, I suppose, as the place was locked up? Still, we might go along and see her when we've had some grub, just on chance.'

He spoke absently, fretted once again by the elusiveness of a fact, retained in his memory, which obstinately refused to surface at the level of consciousness. It was not the basic missing clue, but something somebody had said. Just a casual remark … something…

Suddenly he threw down his pencil. 'Got the street plan handy?' he asked abruptly. 'I've just thought of something.'

Toye produced it, and spread it out.

'You've got the Dibbles' address, haven't you?'

'Oaks Lane,' Toye replied, indicating it on the plan. 'Number Seventeen.'

'How long would it have taken young

Ernie to belt home from Abbot's Green on Wednesday night?'

They worked out the most direct route, and agreed that a boy of Ernie's age could have done it easily in five to six minutes.

'Now, then, how long would it take Mrs Dibble to get home from Escott House?' Pollard asked.

They marked the obvious route on the plan. Toye measured it carefully with a piece of string, which he laid along the scale line. 'Between fifteen and twenty minutes,' he said, after a calculation.

'So, if Billings chucked her out at a quarter to seven pronto, she ought to have got home just after the hour. But Ernie said he just beat her to it, didn't he? He watched Clare Fenner's arrival at five past seven. Say he cleared off at ten past, he'd have arrived home just after quarter-past, which puts his Mum's return at about twenty past. She's got a quarter of an hour unaccounted for. We can rule out prolonged nattering with the other women, as they say they went straight home, or a quick one in a pub – Mrs D. being Mrs D. Shops would be shut. And I shouldn't think she's much of a one for paying social calls, would you?'

'I wouldn't say so,' Toye replied seriously.

'And add to it all that she'd just had words with Billings. Might she have gone back to pay him out somehow? She's one to harbour a grudge all right.'

'I'm not sure you haven't got something there.' Pollard stared at the town plan for a moment. 'She'll probably be more bloody-minded than usual after being in court this morning, but if she was hanging around Escott House anywhere near seven o'clock on Wednesday, I'm going to get it out of her somehow. Let's go and eat first, though.'

Oaks Lane was a drab, nineteenth-century street of working class houses flush to the pavement. Number Seventeen was distinguished from its neighbours by an immaculate doorstep and windows shining with cleanliness. Pollard knocked emphatically on its chocolate brown front door, which was badly in need of a coat of paint.

It was quickly thrown open by Flo Dibble, who stared at him blankly, clearly expecting someone else. She was tidily dressed, in what he guessed was her Sunday best.

'Good afternoon, Mrs Dibble,' he said, before she could speak. 'This visit is nothing whatever to do with Ernie. You remember me? Superintendent Pollard, from Scotland

Yard, down here in Ramsden to inquire into what happened at the Athenaeum. I think you might be able to help us.'

'The probation officer'll be bringing Ernie back any time now,' she said, eyeing Pollard doubtfully.

'We won't keep you more than a few minutes,' he assured her.

'You'd better come inside, then. There's been enough talk b' the neighbours as 'tis.'

In spite of this grudging reception, it struck Pollard that Flo Dibble was in a much more rational frame of mind than when they had met at the police station. He guessed that she had been skilfully handled at the Juvenile Court. They must have realized that, short of removing Ernie from home, nothing could be done for him without remedial work on his mother.

'You must be glad to have somebody to share the responsibility for Ernie,' he remarked, as he followed her into a tiny passage and the front room, with Toye bringing up the rear.

He had hit the right note.

'Thass what the lady and gentleman said,' she replied. 'Time I 'ad a man's 'elp, seein' as the boy's never 'ad a father, in a manner o' speakin'. Done very well, they said I 'ave, keepin' the 'ome together. But 'e mustn't be soft with Ernie, as I tells 'un. Please to sit down.'

The small room managed to be both claustrophobic and bleak. They sat on upright chairs, at a table covered with a green serge cloth. The paint was chocolate brown here, too, and the floor covered with well-scrubbed linoleum. A framed text over the empty grate exhorted them to watch, for they knew not the hour. On a small table in the window a Bible was flanked by an aspidistra.

'It's just this one point, Mrs Dibble,' Pollard began. 'Can you put your mind back to last Wednesday night? You went to work at Escott House as usual, didn't you?'

'That's right, same as usual.'

'What time did you leave?'

Something of the seething indignation that they had witnessed at the police station reasserted itself.

'Quarter to seven. I 'adn't finished me work, and no fault o' mine, seein' there'd bin ink spilt all over the floor in one o' me rooms. But would that Billings wait ten minnits? Not 'im, rarin' mad to git orf to the pub, night after night. 'E's a wine-bibber, an' 'e'll come to no good, as I've told 'n, more 'n once.'

'But if you left Escott House at a quarter to seven, or a minute or two later if you were talking to Billings,' Pollard cut in, as Flo Dibble showed signs of running out of steam, 'how was it that you didn't get back here until about twenty minutes past?'

She looked at him with a gleam of satisfied malice in her hot brown eyes.

'I went back after 'e'd cleared orf, see? I'd slipped the polish and cloths under my coat, so as I could do me brass. That ole brass plate where you goes in, with the funny writin' on it. I keeps n' lovely, an' I wasn't leavin' 'n all mucky, not for a dozen Billingses, no more than I'd leave the door 'andle up to the Athenaeum.'

'Mrs Habgood said this morning how super you make it look,' Pollard told her. 'How long did it take you to go back to Escott House and clean the brass plate?'

Flo Dibble became voluble. She had gone along with her two fellow office cleaners because she didn't want to be laughed at, and that Mrs Doggett was a proper Red over doing a bit extra. As soon as their various ways diverged, she had hurried back to Escott House and got on with the job. She couldn't say to a minute how long it had taken her, but she'd had to wait a bit because she'd heard someone coming ... and then the gate into the car park unlocked ... and she hadn't wanted one of the bosses to see her leaving so late. It was while she was squeezed up in the porch that she'd heard the clocks striking seven, so she couldn't have taken more than five minutes over the brass. Then a car came out – and the gate was locked again – and it was driven off.

'Did it go past the entrance to Escott House, where you were standing?' Toye asked.

'That's right. I watched 'n out of sight an' then skedaddled, not knowin' what the boys 'd be up to, me bein' so late.'

'Did you recognize the driver?' Pollard inquired, as casually as he could.

'Young Mr Escott,' Flo Dibble replied without hesitation. 'I knows 'is car, too. One o' they low-on-the-ground, open sorts.'

'Are you absolutely certain the driver was young Mr Peter Escott?' Pollard pressed her.

'Course I am. I knows 'im orl right. Cleans 'is room, I does, an' a fair muck 'e leave 'n in. 'Ad words with 'im, I 'ave. Not to mention me findin' a book under 'is desk that no decent woman 'd soil 'er hands with. I put 'n straight in the dustbin, I did.'

Pressed yet further, she gestured towards the table in the window, and offered to swear on The Book.

Chapter 11

Within an hour, a white and subdued Peter Escott had left the police station, cleared of responsibility, direct or indirect, for Annabel Brown's death, but informed that a charge of burglary was likely to be brought against him. He had blenched further on being handed a curt written request to drive over to see James Westlake at the latter's house later that evening.

Manifest relief was evident in Superintendent Daly's office, Inspector Cook remarking sardonically that he didn't doubt but that they'd find a way round the theft of the ruddy books.

Over cups of tea and ginger-nuts with Toye, Pollard's immediate reaction was also one of relief. Without Mrs Dibble's conclusive evidence there would have been nothing for it but an interminable search for pedestrians and motorists who might have seen Peter Escott on the previous Wednesday evening. The inquiry would have dragged on and on. Surely it was now perfectly legitimate and reasonable to pack it in? If they started at once on a final report leading up to the formal conclusion of there being insufficient evidence to determine the circumstances of Annabel Brown's death, it would be possible to return to London tomorrow... Fine, except for that niggling conviction that a clue had somehow been overlooked.

Pollard poured himself another cup of tea and drank it down in great gulps, as if trying to drown the niggle.

'There isn't one shred of actual evidence that Brown was blackmailing Mrs Habgood,' he said aloud, a defensive note in his voice. 'And even if there were, there's no proof that she was in on the girl's fall: there never could be any. All we can do is just touch on the bare possibility, in our summing up. If we start now putting the damn thing together, we ought to be through by midday tomorrow.'

Toye, masticating a ginger-nut, nodded without speaking. Pollard looked at him sharply. Blast him, he thought. He knows exactly how I'm feeling. Getting abruptly to his feet, he walked over to the window and stood looking out at the depressing vista of boarded-up houses awaiting demolition. In the half-light of the fading winter day, they looked more dejected than ever. He wondered irrelevantly if Escott's had bought the site and were about to cash in with a property development. By an association of ideas, he found himself visualizing Peter and Evelyn Escott. Then the two Habgoods joined the mental picture, Laura still in the grip of some unexplained, tormenting anxiety. James Westlake presented himself, squared to meet trouble but suddenly looking his age...

In the background there was a rattle of tea cups as Toye began to clear the table for work. Pollard swung round. 'Hell,' he remarked, returning to his chair. 'Sorry to dither, but I've got to have one more bash at the file. Dislike of being done, I suppose. And it's a bit rough on some of these people if it's never cleared up. Don't look so damn' complacent: it's not as though we're going to get anywhere. This missing clue's sunk without trace.'

By half-past then that night, Toye had come to a reluctant agreement. Apart from a short break, they had spent nearly five hours dissecting and discussing the contents of the case file. No fresh lead had emerged. Pollard pushed a pile of papers away and planted his elbows on the table, resting his chin on his clasped hands. In spite of little sleep on the previous night and the effect of prolonged concentration, he felt unusually clear-headed and still quite maddeningly convinced of the existence of the missing clue. For no apparent reason, his mind went back to his first big case: the case of the body in the puppet theatre. On the night when his one remaining lead had petered out he had rung Jane from a telephone kiosk, feeling at rock bottom... And she had urged him to concentrate on the victim, who after all, had somehow sparked off the murder. Then, in some odd way, the stuffy kiosk had become the puppet theatre and he had understood...

Pollard brought his mind back to the present and began to concentrate furiously on Annabel Brown's movements on the evening of her death. She had come out of the Athenaeum with Evelyn Escott; they had paused for a brief moment, then parted, Annabel going into the yard...

'Toye,' he said, so abruptly that the latter gave a start. 'Why the heck have we never given a thought to Brown's car?'

After the excitement of the discovery had subsided, they agreed that the car was unlikely to provide any useful information.

'Could be a letter or a diary,' Toye suggested doubtfully. 'People bung no end of stuff into the dashboard and pockets and forget all about it.'

'We might find a lead to some other blackmailing activities of Brown's, I suppose,' Pollard said, 'but I simply can't believe she was chucked downstairs by somebody we've never heard of up to now. Even the worst detective novels jib at that sort of way out, these days. We'll go along though, even if it's only routine. Let's turn in now. It's been a hellishly long day.'

The garage patronized by Annabel Brown turned out to be a small one in which the owner did the bulk of the work himself. After looking round, Pollard and Toye located a pair of legs protruding from under a car ... and Pollard bent down to introduce himself and his business. The legs made a convulsive movement and a small dark man in an oil-stained boiler suit emerged.

'Sure, that dame's car's here,' he said belligerently, 'and what I want to know is who's paying for the garaging? Over there – the A30. It's all yours.'

He gave a vague gesture, and promptly

dived under the car again.

Pollard and Toye squeezed between other vehicles and through stacks of tyres and various pieces of garage equipment. Toye critically surveyed the A30 and diagnosed rust underneath as he opened the driver's door. A grubby piece of white paper was attached to the steering wheel by string threaded through a hole in one corner.

'Must have car early Saturday morning. Please fill her up as well. A Lucas,' he read aloud.

'It's an old envelope,' Pollard said from behind him. 'Let's have it out.'

Toye carefully untied the string and emerged. The envelope had been slit open and was empty. Annabel Brown's name and address in Moneypenny Street were type-written; and there was a just decipherable London postmark. The date stamp was illegible. There was a printed heading: 'The Queen Alexandra College of Domestic Science, Waverley Road, London NW35Z 1AF'.

'College,' Pollard said, staring at it. 'That piece of carbon paper you found, showing she'd typed something about students. We might have another look at it, I suppose.'

An exhaustive search of the car produced

nothing further of interest; and after brief and unacknowledged thanks to the proprietor of the garage, they returned to the police station.

The carbon paper was unpromising as a source of further information, having been used for making duplicate copies until it was little more than a network of perforations.

'A couple of sheets of glass and a strong light might help,' Pollard said. 'Let's get hold of that bright lad, Neale.'

Detective-Constable Neale eagerly produced these requirements and added a powerful magnifying glass. Pollard sat down at the table and began an inch-by-inch scrutiny of the carbon. After some minutes he muttered something under his breath, and bent forward to peer still more closely.

'Laura, followed by a capital M,' he said, 'Mrs Habgood's maiden name was Marsh. This could be the blackmailing link. Take a look yourself, Toye.'

They finally agreed that nothing more was decipherable.

'If Mrs Habgood went to this college,' Pollard said, making a mental calculation, 'it can't be far short of thirty years ago. Before Brown was born, so how could she – Brown – have got on to anything shady that happened to Mrs H. as a student? Whatever it might have been, you wouldn't think it would be worth much to a blackmailer, after all this time.'

'Suppose Mrs H. was booted out for being pregnant, then produced an illegitimate kid?'

'That's a possibility, of course, especially if Habgood never knew about it. But I still can't think how Brown could have found out.'

They sat in silence, Pollard frowning heavily.

'If there'd been a kid,' Toye said, 'you'd think the Yard would have got on to it when they were getting together that report on her.'

'There wasn't anything to get on to!' Pollard almost shouted, in sudden excitement. 'She never went to this place at all – that's what it is! The report says that she went straight from school into the Wrens. She must have told the Athenaeum people she had a diploma when she hadn't. Now, that's the sort of thing Brown might somehow have found out. I believe we're getting somewhere. We'll ring the Yard and have inquiries made at the College at once.'

After putting this in train, Pollard deliberated for a couple of minutes, then rang

James Westlake.

'I want to ask for some information that you'll probably think absolutely beside the point,' he said. 'Can you think back to 1948, when your Society was appointing its Resident Librarian?'

'Clearly,' James Westlake replied. 'It was a terrific time for RLSS. Crest of the wave, after a shutdown had looked inevitable.'

'Thanks to you and John Donne. Briefly, what was the short list like? What made you decide on Alastair Habgood?'

'There were some good candidates, to answer your first question. We settled for Habgood for several reasons. He had the qualifications, but wasn't too big for the job, if you get me. Psychologically, and also because of his war injury, we felt that the working conditions would suit him. Reasonable tempo, and independence and so on. And, of course, we were influenced by Mrs Habgood's being competent to run the domestic side of the Athenaeum and willing to take it on. She has a domestic science diploma of some sort. Does that answer your second question adequately?'

Pollard thanked him and said that it did. He returned to Toye, and passed on the information.

'We must wait to hear from the Yard,' he said, 'but I think it's reasonable to assume that something conclusive will come through, and there'll be nothing for it but to tackle Mrs Habgood. About the blackmail first, then the implications re Brown's death. Pointless, really, you know. Neither of us can win. Motive or not, we can't prove that she was responsible for it, any more than she can prove that she wasn't. The sort of proof that would stand up in a court of law, I mean. And whether she'd guilty or not, the unfortunate woman will be haunted for the rest of her life, knowing that the inquiry could be reopened at any time.

'Funny that her husband didn't know that she hadn't got this diploma affair,' Toye commented. 'You don't think he was a party to the fraud, do you?'

'I'm certain he wasn't. Men are pretty vague about women's education and, anyway, he'd have been away at the war when she left school and would have been taking the domestic science training for the Diploma, if she'd had one. He'd just accept what she said, when the matter came up.'

'So Brown could have threatened to tell him – rather than Mr Westlake, for instance?'

'This is it, I'm certain. Mrs H. worships

her husband, and Brown knew that she'd got her by the short hairs. What a clever devil she was in her squalid little way, and how I loathe this beastly job of ours. This interview with Mrs H. turns my stomach... Come on, we may as well get cracking on the first part of our report.'

They worked until nearly one o'clock, when the call came through from the Yard. Pollard took it on the extension in their room, jotting down a few notes.

'Briefly,' he told Toye, 'Brown wrote about a year ago to the Alexandra College, saying that she was trying to trace a relative called Laura Marsh, who was believed to have taken a diploma course there, some time between 1945 and 1955. Was this correct, and had the said relative been in touch with them since? They replied that there was no one of that name in their records. On thinking it over,' he went on, after a pause, 'I'll see Laura Habgood on my own. Somehow, I must manage to get her without her husband. I should think he'd be on duty in the library from about two onwards, and it's the sort of time when you would normally find women at home if they don't go out to a job.'

Toye concurred and undertook to be

around with the car about three.

Pollard had timed it well. On his arrival at the Athenaeum he found a notice on the office door directing inquirers for Alastair Habgood to the library. He went upstairs to the flat, unobserved, and rang the bell.

Laura Habgood opened the door. In the moment of confrontation he saw that she knew intuitively why he had come. Without speaking, she stood aside to let him pass, then led the way into the sitting room. Here the initiative passed to himself. He indicated a chair and, when she was seated, took one himself. Laura Habgood, sitting stiffly upright, looked straight at him and asked if he had come to accuse her of killing Annabel Brown.

'If I had, I should have been obliged by law to caution you, Mrs Habgood,' he replied. 'Let's begin at the beginning, shall we? She was blackmailing you, wasn't she?'

Laura nodded but said nothing.

'How did she find out that, when your husband applied for the post here, you falsely claimed to hold a domestic science diploma from the Alexandra College in North London?'

Watching her closely, Pollard saw that his

detailed knowledge had breached her defences.

'If you know all that,' she said slowly, but with an undertone of astonishment, 'I suppose you understand why I did it. I just had to get this job for Alastair. He couldn't have stood up to the ordinary public library. The Trustees interviewed me, too – simply as his wife in the first place – to see if I'd fit. They touched on the domestic problems in a place like this, and and I saw that it might just clinch things if I said I could cope. I was a fool, really. I don't think they cared in the least about my having a diploma. I know it was wrong....' Her voice trailed into silence.

'About Annabel Brown,' Pollard prompted.

'It was a sort of millionth chance... You wouldn't believe it if you read about it. When she first came, we tried to be friendly and make her feel at home; and she was on her best behaviour, of course. There was an RLSS party: she was being rather gushing about the catering in front of some of the members, then suddenly asked if I'd been to a Domestic Science College and taken a diploma. Quite innocently, I think. It was so long ago since that interview that I suppose I may have hesitated – I don't know. Anyway, I rather lost my head and said yes, I'd

287

been to the Alexandra College. It isn't very well known, but I'd just happened to see something about it in the paper a few days before. Well, she'd lived quite near the college and a cousin had been there.'

Laura Habgood broke off, twisting her fingers nervously and looking at him with wretchedness in her eyes.

'So I suppose she began asking questions and caught you out?' Pollard asked.

'Yes. And a few weeks later she brought me a letter from the college saying I'd never been there, and started blackmailing me.'

'Threatening to tell your husband?'

Once more, Laura nodded affirmatively without speaking. Pollard allowed a pregnant silence to build up.

'When you went out to the gallery last Wednesday night,' he said abruptly, 'what exactly was Annabel Brown doing?'

She stared at him blankly. 'I don't understand. You know I never went into the library.'

'I know that you deny having gone in,' he replied. 'Not quite the same thing, is it? I repeat, *what was she doing?*'

He watched her drag her hand over her hair in a desperate gesture. 'But I didn't – I swear I didn't. You're trying to make me in – incriminate myself. It's wicked!– Don't you want the truth?'

'I'll tell you what she was doing, Mrs Habgood,' Pollard went on, disregarding her reply. 'She was at the cupboard that had been broken open, helping herself to some valuable books. You startled her and she came towards you. You met at the top of the spiral staircase, didn't you?'

The initial shock of his changed tactics had passed, he saw, and something of her robustness of character had returned to her.

'I repeat,' she said steadily, 'I didn't go into the library again after I locked it up on Wednesday evening. I swear it.'

He went on questioning her with unrelenting pressure, but her denials remained absolute and consistent. His conviction that she was speaking the truth mounted steadily. Finally, he broke off as abruptly as he had begun, and tried the often effective catalyst of sudden sympathy.

'I'm sorry to have distressed you like this,' he said, getting to his feet and looking down on her. 'I'm afraid it's part of my job.'

She began to cry quietly, but showed no sign of capitulating from exhaustion and sudden relief of tension.

'If only you'd say you believe me,' she said unsteadily.

'Speaking as a fellow human being,' Pollard told her, 'I do. As a police officer I can only report to my superiors that you had motive and ample opportunity to push Annabel Brown down that staircase, but that there is no evidence that you did.'

'And Alastair? You couldn't – couldn't be so cruel,' she burst out.

'On that score,' he assured her, 'you don't have to worry.'

Laura sank back in her chair, as he picked up his brief-case and went out of the room. He stood briefly on the landing, coming to terms with the inescapable fact that he had reached the end of the road. Perhaps, he told himself, the elusive missing clue had been disguised chagrin at finding himself up against an insoluble problem...

From the hall downstairs came the un-mistakable sound of Alastair Habgood's footsteps, going to the office. On impulse Pollard opened the door on to the gallery and stood looking down. The library was empty. An Anglepoise lamp made a pool of light on the books and papers on the librarian's table. In the bays, the afternoon shadows were gathering, but across the great room the portrait of the first Evelyn Escott stood out boldly in its massive gilt frame.

Pollard contemplated its purposeful ebullience, wondering if the original had ever been forced to concede defeat.

There were voices in the distance. Pollard listened, and identified that of Toye, who must have arrived with the car and be talking to Alastair Habgood in the office. It was essential not to give the impression of having come from the flat. Pollard tiptoed hastily along the gallery to the spiral staircase.

Without warning several things seemed to happen simultaneously. He trod on something soft and yielding, yet animate, which pushed between his feet with an eldritch screech, throwing him off balance. Encumbered by the brief-case he was carrying, he grasped ineffectively at the rail, saving himself from a headlong descent but falling awkwardly, with his left leg bent under him. An agonizing pain shot through him and for a couple of seconds everything blacked out. He surfaced to the sound of running feet and found himself looking into Toye's horrified face.

'Bloody cat,' he heard himself gasp. 'Tripped me up. I think I've bust my leg.'

There were other arrivals. Alastair Habgood was beside Toye, and he could sense Laura's presence on the upper part of the staircase. A pillow was slipped under his head, which had been pressing uncomfortably against a tread, and a rug was lowered over him. He caught the word 'ambulance'. It had an instantly clarifying effect. In a flash, a series of hitherto unrelated facts resolved themselves into a meaningful pattern. He seized on the immediate priority.

'To hell with an ambulance,' he told Toye forcibly. 'Get these trousers off before I'm carted away, and take 'em to the forensic lab with Brown's jeans. Tell 'em to vet the bottoms of the legs with everything they've got ... I don't care what the ambulance chaps say – *this is an order, man...*'

In spite of the ambulance men's skill, being transferred to a stretcher was damnable. Pollard managed to drag out a handkerchief and wipe his face.

'Don't have the little perisher put down,' he said, giving Alastair Habgood a weak grin as he was borne away.

Laura seemed to have assumed that she would accompany him to the hospital. As the ambulance moved off, he reflected that he must surely be the first CID Super to travel in one, minus trousers, and escorted by a woman whom he had just interviewed in connection with a potential homicide charge.

'Nice, clean fracture of the left tibia,' the Casualty Officer said, studying the X-ray plates. 'We'll soon have you fixed up, old man...'

The missing clues – Pollard quickly realized that there was more than one – had surfaced during the tedious sojourn in the X-ray department. What mattered now was the report from the forensic lab, to clinch everything. At intervals, during the process of being admitted to a ward and cleaned up for the theatre, he emphasized to various medical personnel the vital importance of Inspector Toye's being allowed immediate access to him at all times. The bright and soothing reassurances he received struck him as unconvincing. There was nothing he could do about it, though, and after his pre-med jab it began to seem less important...

Once or twice during the night the pain in his leg woke him, but somebody was there to do something about it, and everything drifted away again. Then it was broad daylight and he was in bed in an unfamiliar small white room. He gingerly explored the armour plating encasing his left leg, and with relief spied a telephone on his locker. They must have put him in a private room.

The door was half open, and a blonde head came round it, topped by a vestigial cap.

'Awake at last?' a young voice inquired perkily. 'I'll tell Sister.'

Sister momentarily took him aback: with-it hairdo, eye-shadow, lipstick. *Plus ça change,* though, he thought, under the impact of her competently assessing eye and her bracing information on his progress and prospects. He learned with astonishment that he might be allowed to stand, briefly, later in the day. Mr Wilkinson-Croft, his surgeon, would be looking in during the morning.

He also gathered that he had status, and it told... He might like to ring Mrs Pollard right away, before nurse straightened him up for breakfast. Inspector Toye? Well, the rule was no morning visitors, of course, but under the circumstances... Yes, he had called already, and said he would be back within the hour...

Blast him, Pollard thought, dialling the Wimbledon number. Why hadn't he left a note? No news, good news?

Jane's voice came through. 'Hallo, darling,' he said, instantly translated to another world. 'Well, apparently you're not going to be tied to a helpless cripple for life, after all... No, absolutely all right. Good as new...

294

Yes, by the end of the week, Sister says...
Physiotherapy when the plaster's off... This
is it: sick leave plus leave due...'

As they talked, a broken leg – the sort of
disaster that happened to other people –
began to fit into the context of everyday life.
The conversation moved on discreetly to
the case.

'All but home and dry,' Pollard told her.
'I'm lying in bed sweating with impatience
for old Toye to come in with the final tie-up.
I'm wondering,' he went on, after her
delighted exclamation, 'if you could possibly
do with an addition to the household? Cat,
small, black, friendly, answering to the name
of Nox. I suspect he's going to be considered
too much of a hazard by his present owners.
Have you got him there, by any chance?'

There was a pause, and a gasp of astonishment.

'How absolutely right I was!' Jane asserted
triumphantly.

'Right about what?'

'You being newsworthy, of course. A sort
of publicity lightning conductor. This'll hit
the headlines for six! Animals in the news go
straight to the Great British Public's head.'

Pollard was assailed by a horrific vision,
which included the reactions of the AC and

his colleagues to any development of the sort. 'Rot,' he said, with less than his usual conviction. 'I don't suppose a fiddling little job like this will make the papers at all.'

Jane chortled. 'Oh, yeah? Let me tell you that I've had two newsmen on the line already this morning. If I'm wrong,' she went on, in the confident ring of someone betting on a certainty, 'I'll stand you a night out on my first earnings.'

Duly straightened up for his breakfast, Pollard, his tension returned, poked half-heartedly at scrambled eggs. His ear was cocked for every footstep in the corridor. Who the hell were all the people who kept passing, he wondered impatiently? When the door suddenly opened he was momentarily speechless with his mouth full of toast, and could only stare at the neat, horn-rimmed figure who stood giving the V-sign.

'For God's sake come in and shut the door,' he said indistinctly, swallowing painfully.

Toye carried out these instructions and came up to the bed. Pollard realized that he was valiantly struggling to conceal emotion.

'I'm OK,' he said. 'Let's have it.'

'Home and dry, sir,' Toye told him. 'Identical hairs on both garments, on the inner side of the bottoms of the legs. Identical with the samples Neale got from the staircase treads, and with the cat's. I took him along for a test this morning.'

They looked at each other in silent jubilation.

'Here, dump this beastly tray outside, somewhere,' Pollard said, 'and we may get a few minutes' peace. If they try to winkle you out, I'll start talking about the Assistant Commissioner, who I know so well, like an outraged upper-class suspect. You've rung his office, I take it?'

'Yes, sir,' Toye replied, having got rid of the tray. 'I'm to go up this afternoon with a full report. He'll be ringing you personally, his secretary said. And I've passed all the information on to Inspector Cook.'

As he spoke, he pulled up a chair and they settled down in the effortless intimacy built up over years of working together.

'Let's face it,' Pollard said. 'We missed out all along the line. Preconceived assumptions, I suppose. I got it all sorted out while I was hanging around in the X-ray department last night. Going right back to the start, I remember spotting the cat ladder when we went round the yard after we arrived, but it didn't really register. One's mind was on the boiler house door.'

'Not the sort of thing you'd give any weight to,' Toye insisted loyally.

'All the same, it was part of the set-up. Well, we then had Habgood's statement that the cat Nox landed on his chest, accompanied by the row of the electric beater at about five to seven on Wednesday evening. Last Sunday we had a clear hint that the animal is allergic to that sort of noise. Remember how he came out from under the sofa in the library when Mrs H. switched off the Hoover?'

Toye nodded, too absorbed for speech.

'Right. Now, obviously Nox was in the library when Brown came back there on Wednesday evening. Either he got shut in by mistake at closing time or slipped in from the yard, both Escott and Brown having left the door open for a quick exit. Cats are nosy creatures. Can't you picture Nox, invisible in the dark, stalking Brown as she crawled around and finally went up to the gallery? The circle of light from her torch must have fascinated him, and he would have taken up an observation post on the spiral staircase. Then she starts to come down. Her arms are full of books and she finds it difficult to focus her torch properly. Quite suddenly, Ernie lets the latch of the main door drop, and she thinks someone is coming in. She panics, takes a hasty step in the dark, and treads on Nox. He is terrified and trips her up just as he did me last night, only she isn't quick enough to grab and rail and save herself. Nox gives the screech reported by Ernie, then belts for the yard and his ladder to home and friends. But when he fetches up in the flat, he's greeted by the electric beater going full blast. It's more than he can take, and he rushes to his master for protection.'

'But he'd got to get into the boiler house through that fake door,' Toye objected.

'This is it. We didn't give that door enough attention, either. I did examine it, being keen on old buildings, but as with the cat ladder, the important point about it didn't register. It's only painted wood, fastened by a small unobtrusive catch on the library side, which Escott would have undone when he put away the stacking chairs. There was a very small risk that someone would notice this on Wednesday, but his luck held. Things were a bit at sixes and sevens the next day, with Habgood out of action. But when the door into the yard was open, the draught would make the fake door swing to and fro.

Not much, but enough for a frantic cat to claw its way out.'

'Ernie's door, shutting "quiet like"?'

'Just that. By the way, what have you done with Nox?'

Toye, temporarily lost in admiration, roused himself. 'I delivered him back to the Athenaeum. Mr and Mrs Habgood are in a proper taking. They say he'll have to go, after what's happened. They can't risk any more accidents on the spiral staircase. Put to sleep if they can't find a good home for him. They asked me to tell you, since you'd made a point of it.'

'All fixed,' Pollard replied, cautiously shifting his position and eyeing the door, outside which a group discussion was building up. 'Tell them my wife and I will cherish him for the rest of his nine lives, if they'd like us to take him on. The kids are animal mad. I can–'

The door was purposefully opened. A nurse entered, carrying a basket of fruit.

'I'm sorry, Superintendent Pollard, but Sister says Mr Wilkinson-Croft will be along any time now – this has just come for you.'

'All right, Nurse. Inspector Toye, you'd better clear out for the moment. Come back as soon as possible and we'll finish that report for the Assistant Commissioner. I shall want you here for the rest of the morning, of course.' He winked outrageously at Toye behind the nurse's back.

'Here, this is right up your street,' he added, as she went out again, leaving the door open.

Together they read the label attached to the basket of fruit. It conveyed the joint wishes of Evelyn M. Escott and James R. F. Westlake, for a speedy recovery.

A slow smile lit up Toye's face. 'I reckon he's spoken,' he said.

This Large Print Book, for people
who cannot read normal print,
is published under the auspices of

THE ULVERSCROFT FOUNDATION